No Sound to Break,
No Moment Clear

ALSO BY STEFAN KIESBYE

Berlingeles

But I Don't Know You

Cover Stories

Knives, Forks, Scissors, Flames

Next Door Lived A Girl

The Staked Plains

Your House Is on Fire, Your Children All Gone

No Sound to Break,
No Moment Clear

A NOVEL

Stefan Kiesbye

BRIGHTHORSE
BOOKS

Brighthorse Books
13202 N River Drive
Omaha, NE 68112
brighthorsebooks.com

ISBN: 978-1-944467-31-9

For permission to reproduce selections from this book for purposes other than review, contact the editors at info@brighthorsebooks.com. Brighthorse books are distributed to the trade through Ingram Book Group and its distribution partners. To learn more about Brighthorse Books, go to brighthorsebooks.com.

For Juvenal and Sanaz

I want to go with the one I love.
I do not want to calculate the cost.
I do not want to think about whether it's good.
I do not want to know whether he loves me.
I want to go with whom I love.

— Bertolt Brecht

No Sound to Break,
No Moment Clear

Our town once stood on an island in the middle of Lake Superior. The outcropping was a mile long and a smidge more than a mile across, a near perfect square. The first congregation of huts served as a trading post—furs from the north, liquor and dried goods from the south. The island provided a harbor for ships crossing the ocean lake, a natural harbor fortified by Finnish settlers. Rough seas turned it deadly; ships ran aground or crashed into the rocks. During winter storms, no sane person attempted to land.

A hundred years later, no town was left. The island had sunk back into the lake and soon after, it disappeared from the maps as well. The water had threatened the doorsteps of the settlers for years. Everybody knew what had to be done, and the long debates after dark with whiskey and dried meats only served to make the unthinkable less daunting. If they could talk about it, they would find a way to imagine it. In the end, there was less time left than they had hoped.

The townspeople set toward the south where they had bought land from a band of Chippewa. One of the schooners, the Frederique, carried livestock—goats and reindeer and seven cows and thirty-seven chickens and four sheep, according to the ledger still displayed behind glass at Sparcky's. It hangs beyond the counter made from the planks of the Frederique. As a boy, I ran my hands over the wood and cried, I wanted to see the lost island so badly.

The Pity, the biggest ship, held twenty-three passengers and their belongings, plus the trading post's stock of furs and liquor. The other boats lost sight of her after nightfall. No storm threatened the small fleet; the winds had been friendly all week. Yet the Pity disappeared, and its twenty-three passengers and their belongings with it. All that was ever found, months later, was the upper part of the figurehead, a scantily-clad woman covering her face with her hands.

My grandmother Anna Holmstrom, nee Tuomainen, whose family could trace its roots to those early days of our town, told me that story first. She always ended with, "I feel that's all you need to know, until this world ends, and the lake freezes solid." She'd lost her great-great-great-uncle when the Pity sank. My grandfather Frank never questioned the story when she was present.

The sense of destiny that the legend of the rocky island bestowed on our small town had faded by the time I was a teenager, turned threadbare, see-through. Only Trunk House, a small building at the end of Grant Street, exhibited artifacts from the first settlers in two of its rooms. Old bottles, knives, discolored letters. Long before my parents bought their house, the town devised the slogan, "Our Town—Your Destination for Work and Play," and to attract travelers, they cleaned up the municipal airport and installed a shuttle to Marquette. This was an eighteen-seat turbo-prop plane, twenty years old, and it connected the world to our new convention center, built on twenty acres of land half a mile south of our high school. The building's facade recalled the prow of a schooner, complete with the figurehead of the Pity, but beyond the foyer it was all concrete rectangles. A Cineplex and a mall flanked the center.

After four years, the Church of Latter-day Saints moved into the structure, and after that, the local AA group and the chess club held meetings in one of the smaller conference rooms. By the time my voice became a mess, nobody set foot in our town's future anymore. What we were left with was winter, his presence so solid you never forgot about him, not even at the height of summer; his scent nested in women's hair and their flowing garments, he made men set their jaws.

1

After the first days, we stopped shoveling. The wind had picked up and blew the snow sideways, transferring mounds from there to here, filling in our lanes from porch to street, and creating valleys in random places. Our town grew soft bellies and ridged spines, white legs and backs slung together. Traffic stopped and the phone lines went dead; next fall, the pastor said, he'd be baptizing the results of the whiteout, no one less beautiful or more special than the next. This was in the early days of the storm, when people's pantries were still stacked high with food and the power was still on. Wood was plenty and the smoke from fireplaces and stoves kept the houses visible even after snow was reaching the roofs and rendering windows useless.

The storm picked up force on the twenty-fifth, after Katia and I opened the presents my parents had sent from overseas, wrapped in cloth and held together with green yarn, and she made breakfast because she was three years older and supposed to look out for me. "I'm not your mom, I'm better than that," she said several times a day. "A girl's not a beast." Katia was seventeen and a junior in high school. My voice squeaked and burst when I got serious or excited, but Katia had long stopped pointing it out, she only rolled her eyes. It wasn't funny anymore to her, or maybe it reminded her of how lonely she was in my parents' house and how much she missed Lucas, her boyfriend, who had left town to go to a college several hundreds of miles south and who hadn't come home for the holidays. Even I knew what that meant, but Katia didn't talk about Lucas' absence. It was a rite of passage, neighbors said when she wasn't around. A heart needed to be broken to stand a chance in this world.

Katia's face was framed by pimples who received better care than the books she read or the meals she prepared for us. Much of our food came from cans. Mom and Dad had left a large roll of dollar bills in a jar that had once held polish for Mom's silver and Dad's watch from the war. They had counted out the money one night, explained that we needed to be frugal and disciplined, but that we would be fine. Opa Frank next door would still be around. Could they count on us? they asked, and we knew what they expected and nodded gravely, whitewash lies. Dad's hair was wispy and growing sparse in back. Mom's mouth was small and lined as though it had been cut from bark. She still had her teeth, but she never showed them, not even when she was smiling.

In October they left on their mission. They would go to Africa and later to Southeast Asia, wherever they were needed. Dad had quit his job as foreman at the slaughterhouse; Mom had cried after coming home on her final day as receptionist in Dr. Koren's office. The doctor had agreed to treat me and Katia should we need his help. So far, we hadn't even come down with a cold. We weren't babies anymore, our parents had kept reminding us, and we both held ourselves with new stern expressions. Our bodies seemed to have grown stiffer and heavier with the new responsibility for our lives. Katia cut her own hair these days and shore off mine when it grew past my ears. She asked me to take off my clothes and bend my head over the bathroom sink. Once or twice the blade caught my ear, but she apologized every time. I liked her attention, which she only offered when my body needed food or maintenance. I pretended to have splinters in my fingers or a burning sensation in my lower back. Katia inspected without complaining.

Every night, she counted out the dollar bills, large fingers stroking the money that said we were alone in this house, that the only noise we heard was the noise we made, sounds speaking of a new ease. We no longer had anything to hide. I wanted to can the sound of her feet descending the stairs, her fingers scratching her head, the humming when she swept the kitchen.

Katia said, "If they die, they'll bury them there. We'll never get to see them."

"We don't see them right now," I said.

Katia slapped the back of my head, she was crying. "They left us, and they could be gone without a trace that they ever existed."

"But we remember them. We know they were there."

"But their faces are already blurry, and we don't know what they look like right now. We don't know them."

The mail wasn't delivered anymore, or else we didn't get any. We had received a card from our uncle out west, and another from our one remaining grandmother, our dad's mother, who lived near the gulf. She had enclosed small gifts for us, socks and gloves, and some money. With a few of our parents' bills, Katia bought me a die-cast model plane, and I gave her perfume that was supposed to smell like something we couldn't afford. The plane was a Russian MiG and not one of my favorites; the perfume smelled citrusy and not unlike the dish soap Mom used to buy. We hugged and said thank you, and we hadn't had breakfast yet and her breath smelled bad and her neck was warm. She said I needed to put on clean pajamas.

Our backyard we hadn't set foot in since the beginning of the storm. Beyond a fence with sagging and broken panels, the dark expanse of forest we called Siberia turned bright white and glassy when the sun appeared for a brief moment before being swallowed whole again. The trees had laid down their leaves so recklessly.

The steps to our porch disappeared, and I stopped visiting my friend Miles, the only one who invited me to birthday parties and whose mom let me stay for dinner. Yet once a day, Katia and I wrested open the front door and I crawled into the snow toward where our mailbox was no longer visible. Every time I returned empty-handed with a red face and sweaty clothes despite the cold. We knew the ritual to be senseless—it took me minutes to locate the post and more minutes to tear open the frozen latch—and yet it felt absolutely necessary, like eating and sleeping and reading stories to each other. On the twenty-seventh, our grandfather's lights next door again failed to come on after dark. It was the fourth day in a row, unusual even for him.

We hadn't received any presents from Opa Frank, nor had he come over to check on us for Christmas. He always left on short trips for the weekend. Ever since his wife had died some eight years prior, he'd been leaving Friday night more often than not, to return Sunday night or Monday morning to open his office. Rumor had it that he'd acquired a lady friend down south. Mom thought he just needed to get out of town; too much reminded him of his loss.

Oma Anna had been the first dead person I had laid eyes on. Her open casket had stood at Mancuso's funeral home for two days, and Mom had insisted we go and see her. She had shoved us toward the dead body and made us watch her as she kissed her mother's face. I'd been five and thinking about the bags of candy I wouldn't receive anymore. The last one wasn't even empty yet, and I swore, right there in front of the casket, that I wouldn't touch a single chocolate. Opa stood to the side, his hands around other people's hands, other people's hands around his. "I'm sorry for your loss," I kept mumbling for days. Opa's eyes were red-rimmed, his shoes so highly polished they reflected the dim light coming from the candelabra.

Since then, Mom had invited him to dinner once a month, yet even on evenings he did show up, he found ways to cut the visit short. He'd chew his food and say to my dad, "Bill, there's no such thing as reformed Egyptian." Or he'd gnaw on a chicken bone and ask, "Bill, how did the Jaredites get to America?" After a glass of wine, he'd stage-whisper, with a wink in my mother's direction, "Bill, when will you be able to afford a few more wives?" I laughed because I thought I was supposed to.

Dad said little in return, waiting as for a low-flying Starfighter to pass and quiet to resume. By the end of the night, his features looked tired. He didn't have a degree from medical school, he wasn't a respected pediatrician. Opa Frank—and the old man never failed to mention it—had given them money for the down payment of the house. Without him, Dad couldn't have supported his daughter properly.

"We should check on him," Katia said. "We haven't heard from him at all." She'd served dinner at around seven, a departure from our parents' routine. They never ate later than six o'clock and insisted on us staying seated until everyone had emptied their plates. Each night, one of us had to say blessings, and we couldn't take salad or potatoes before Dad had served himself. But with our parents gone, we changed dinner time, and we didn't say blessings any longer. Instead, we recited nursery rhymes or lines from our favorite songs. We also burnt incense sticks—an extravagance Katia had insisted on.

"We haven't seen him in weeks," Katia remarked after I pointed at the dark house through the kitchen window. I had cleared the table and was doing our dishes, which sometimes took me thirty minutes. Not because we dirtied that many, but I would fill one of the sinks with soapy water, the other with clean one, and then I would sail paper boats or watch the bubbles turn color before finally popping. It wasn't that interesting, really, but more interesting than scraping mashed potatoes from a pot or trying to undo the damage from burnt sauce, burnt meat, or burnt beans. I dreamed of snake pits, lost cities, and nude beaches. Soaking helped and sidetracked me for many more minutes.

"Did you see any lights last night?" I asked.

"No. But the day before Christmas Eve I did see the one in his bedroom. And in the living room. He was definitely there that night."

Together we stared at the dark window on the second floor behind which lay his bedroom. Snow clung to the lower half of the house, obliterating the windows. We would have noticed light behind them.

"Maybe he left," I said.

"We should check the garage. See if the driveway has been shoveled."

"Maybe someone picked him up."

"Who would that be, potato face?" She called me that whenever I thought aloud. "Mom says we're his only family."

I stared again at the dark windows. The water for the dishes had long turned cold. The silverware still lay at the bottom of the sink. The silverware was always last—knives and forks were terrible to clean. The skin of my fingers was shriveled and white and the thought of touching any more dishes disgusted me. "I can go over and knock on his door if you do the rest."

She checked the sink and said, "Okay."

I pulled on a second pair of pants, slipped into my dad's winter boots, buttoned my stiff coat, and grabbed woolen mitts. This time we had to pour hot water on the frame for the door to open. While Katia cleaned up the mess, I dove into the snow. The distance to Opa Frank's porch was about twenty yards, but the snow now reached my shoulders, and I grew panicked in the dark, as though I could get lost or lose the ability to move. Maybe my body heat would melt the snow enough for it to freeze around me seconds after I stopped struggling, and I'd be preserved, silent and blind, until spring. Above me, there was no sky, only more snow, more ice. I was stuck between two houses and still I was nowhere, swept away by storm and ice, dragged away from our town and Katia.

I bumped my head on Opa's bannister, clung to the wood, and worked my way up. On the porch, I could finally catch my breath. I saw Katia standing at our kitchen window and waved, and she waved back.

Opa Frank's door had not been opened in a while—there were no new footprints other than mine on the porch, only old, re-filled ones, and the accumulated snow around door and frame was pristine. I rang the doorbell, or thought I did, but I couldn't hear a sound from within the house. So I reached up and knocked against the glass, which I feared would splinter into pieces, then beat against the wood. I waited, and my sweat grew cold. I jumped up and down, but nothing happened.

"What do you want me to do?" I screamed at our lighted kitchen window, but whatever Katia responded mixed with the whistling snow and never reached me. I tried the door knob and pulled with all my strength, but the door didn't budge. I shouted with my breaking voice until it gave out. If Opa was at home, he wasn't aware of my efforts. I looked up and down our street. Several streetlights had given up, and none of our neighbors were outside.

Before I stepped off the porch, I saw the woman. She was not much taller than me. She was wearing a wool dress and shiny pumps. Her face was as red as my own, her breath white like my own. I didn't think her pretty.

The lack of a coat or mittens or hat struck me as curious. Her fingers curled around the railing as though she wanted to tear it away, or else cling to it for dear life. I had never seen her before; I wasn't afraid. In response to her urgency I lifted my arms, unwound my scarf and held it out to her. Before I could take off my gloves, she had slipped back into the storm and turned invisible. When I looked at the spot where she had stood, her footsteps were already losing their contours.

I hoped that Katia had finished the dishes by now. Maybe she'd made hot chocolate.

•

At the start, every day was Sunday; we'd moved into our parents' bedroom on the spot. Katia and I divided the house among us for daytime use—she chose the upstairs bathroom; mine was the downstairs one—and we followed our own rules. We had moved the dining table into the living room; the dining room had become the place where Katia did her gymnastics or drew cartoons while lying on the floor and listening to people strumming acoustic guitars. At night, though, we enjoyed the luxury of the extra space, the wide bed, the matching nightstands and reading lamps, and the softness of the down comforters. Daylight diminished the bedroom—this was not a room for any specific use other than sleeping and storing clothes. Nobody lived in here, one only slept. Daylight rendered the room a mausoleum, but at night, the reading lamps threw so many shadows that the space seemed cavernous and full of secrets. The closets stopped smelling of mothballs, and Katia and I often dressed with what our parents had left behind. I preferred my father's green military coat, which nearly fit me and which felt tent-like, something to crawl into and hide from enemies. My dad also owned a fur cap with a Russian red star attached to its front flap, and I'd sit propped against the pillows and read one of the tomes my mother dusted once a week meticulously and without feeling. These days I read *A Good Woman*, not understanding the time or context. Still, the book filled me with a new confidence, an anticipation of things to come. I couldn't know what they were, yet they made my limbs tingle. I was growing at an alarming rate.

More often than not, my sister chose one of my mother's three or four evening dresses. We'd never seen her wearing any of these. They had no sleeves, were made of shiny and colorful fabrics. One was pure gold, and Katia looked very expensive in it. She bemoaned the fact that her breasts were already larger than Mom's and flattened against the fabric; her hips didn't fit the slim cut. "I look humongous," she said and kept wearing the gold dress anyway. Around her shoulders she draped a fur stole, which smelled horrible but was so soft I kept stroking it.

"What should we do?" I asked later that night. "He might be dead." Tonight I was wearing a leather cap my dad had used during the time he owned a motorcycle. I wore the leather jacket as well, even though it was very heavy and stiff and not particularly warm. I hadn't told Katia about the woman on our grandfather's porch. I could no longer remember her face. She hadn't said a word.

"He might have money in his mattress." Katia got up for the fourth or fifth time and regarded herself in the mirror. "I'm thinking I'm in a different category now. Not worse, necessarily, but narrower in terms of people who will find me interesting. We're all just headed for death. You should try this on," she said.

"Maybe he has guns or gold coins." I got up from the bed and took off jacket and cap. Katia peeled out of the dress and handed it to me. She didn't even notice I was staring at her.

"If he's sick, we need to call the hospital," she said.

"If I wear the dress, you wear this." I handed her the jacket and cap, then went to the closet and extracted one of Dad's army pants. "The lines are dead. We'll have to get help in town."

"It's terrible to talk about him like that when we're only a few steps away." Katia buttoned the leather jacket and pulled up her hair and stuffed it into the cap. "Last Christmas he gave you one of his old toy trains."

"I'm fourteen," I said. "I don't play with that stuff anymore." Mom's dress was lined and silky inside, though the gold fabric was rough to the touch. "Can you zip me?" I asked in a high voice and turned my back to her.

Mom's shoes were too small for me, but I was able to squeeze into a pair of her sandals. Katia looked for a scarf and wound it around my head. "How do I look?" Not waiting for an answer, I stepped in front of the large silver mirror and stared. Katia joined me. We stayed quiet for a long time. The floorboards creaked without us moving, and we felt the wind scraping along the windows.

"You're really pretty," she finally said. "The dress fits you much better than me."

I didn't say that my father's pants fit her perfectly, though it was true. Under the stiff leather, I could hardly make out her breasts, and her hair was hidden. In the soft light of our reading lamps, her acne turned into the shadow of a beard. Katia looked very much like Dad. I resembled my mom. We both recognized that, I'm sure of it, and we both said nothing. This was our game, the winner a cheat whose mind's on other things. Moments later, Katia turned to me, took my face in both her hands and kissed me for the first time. "My light remains flickering in winter," she whispered. "I hold your breath and you are holding mine." I had never felt a tongue in my mouth before, but I didn't squirm, just received. I understood that this was her moment, not mine. She bit my lower lip, and I whimpered in response. She tightened her grip around my neck, pulled back my head by getting hold of the scarf. Then her fingers, hard and comforting, wrote softly through my hair. The other hand squirmed down my back and came to rest on my butt. "You have a hard-on," she said.

.

Logic holds no sway over my emotions. I am just a tenant here, living in and out of this life as cheaply as I can. I move away from a bum sitting in the doorway of a downtown building in fear I might suffer the same fate. Poverty is not an infectious disease, but my mind won't be convinced. Before every meal I join my hands, not in prayer but to be *ready*. Life ends after our death—there is no second act, no white light at the end of the tunnel, no rebirth as a German Shepherd. I have accepted this, yet I also side with the Hindu religion—we have stages to fulfill and won't be released from our human form until we have lived enough lives to complete our obligations. I don't put my hat on my bed.

You can call it superstition, you can accuse me of a feeble imagination, of a lack of discipline in my thoughts. These I have been tagged with before. Still, a stringent imagination strikes me as no imagination at all, and to get rid of the contradictions in my thoughts would also mean losing the darker spots in my mind where broom and wet cloth can't reach and make life possible. Do we not need unobserved spaces, spaces where we can be victim and perpetrator at the same time, dictator and prey, strong and vulnerable in equal measure?

Which of my actions were permissible? Which will be denounced? I laid down among murderers. I tended to love carelessly, looked upon nature with impatience. As a boy I read for guidance, didn't want to get swept away, needed proof that rules existed for good reason. In the end, I found that each thought is canceled out by its exact opposite, both true, and I know less every year. What I have done in the time that was given me has barely left a trace. All the while, the planet is overburdened, was overburdened already during the winter when Katia and I grew worried about Opa Frank and tried on our parents' clothes and discovered we couldn't pass muster. Were we wrong?

To think that our white wooden houses and churches, our weapons and inventions, will buy us time is vanity. We are killing this planet—we extend our lives and breed and multiply. We start our own families, our own nightmares. Unwilling to stop giving life, we give death instead. Logic has nothing to do with our actions. How could my life have been any different?

I'm lost, she was never there. It's always the same.

·

We never switched off the lights in those days, our windows never bright enough for us to read. The storm made our doors and roof sing; the heat was always on high. Katia made breakfast the next morning, her mood especially foul. This was the way she punished herself, her way of letting me know we had gone too far. By now I recognized the pattern.

After eating and clearing away the plates in silence we put on coats and boots. Our side door, too, was frozen shut, and after using a hairdryer along the edges and pulling until we thought we might break off the handle, snow blew its way into the house, a curious intruder. Wet prints appeared everywhere. "Did you see his car last night?" Katia asked.

I shook my head. I'd been too afraid to prolong my search

and venture toward the garage. "What if we can't get back in? If our door freezes shut?" I said.

Katia shrugged. "You want to stay, potato face?"

Dimmed daylight rubbed more ice and snow in our faces. The storm hadn't let up, not even for an hour. We couldn't see our neighbors across the street, and they couldn't see us. We were quarantined on a distant planet trying to get rid of us. This time I tried not to panic, not to work too hard to make my way across to our grandfather's house, but no matter. Within a few minutes my face glowed hot and my shirt was soaked with sweat.

The garage door was locked, no tracks visible. The small window was crusted with ice—we couldn't determine whether Opa's car was inside or not.

The kitchen door in back was our only chance. If Opa Frank had left it unlocked we'd be able to get inside. Neither Katia nor I wished to break a window and climb through the opening, though the snow reached up high enough in places to make it easy. What would we say when he confronted us, coming down the stairs to see what the ruckus was all about? How would we explain? How would we pay for the damage?

We removed the snow in front of the door as best we could—there were shovels in our garage, but the garage door was frozen shut—then pushed, and I lost my balance and Katia fell on top of me. For a moment we lay still, listening into the silence. I thought I heard the house breathing; it was expecting us. Steam was coming off Katia's hat and coat. "Opa Frank," she called out, then coughed violently, cleared her throat, tried again.

The house smelled odd. Not of food or pine needles or wet woolens, more like an empty garage, like dark soil, like things in old glass bottles without labels, like chalk. I'd always looked forward to visiting Oma Anna when she was still alive; hers had been a cozy place, not cluttered like our own. She had been an imposing figure back then, taller than her husband, stern, yet handing out candy or money every chance she got. Except for the smell, little had changed since her death; her absence hung about. If you reached out your hand, you touched what was missing. On my final visit, days before she died, she promised me, "I will always be with you," and I stole into my sister's bed that night, hands and feet full of ice.

We picked ourselves off the floor and looked around the kitchen. Cups were sitting by the sink, smeared with coffee. Bread had been left out in its plastic bag. A jar of jelly stood next to it. Otherwise, the surfaces were well-mannered and clean. "Opa," I crowed. Until sixth grade, I had sung in school choir. My voice had been clear and cold, and listening to my echo now, I detested what had become of it. I was wet and freezing in my clothes and felt like the opposite of my grandfather's kitchen. I was sprouting hair all over my body, and everyone could hear what a mess I was. "Opa Frank." My voice ended in an odd whistle, and despite the situation and her mood, Katia laughed. Then she came to my help and shouted the old man's name.

Moving toward the front of the house, we saw that the thermostat was set to fifty-six degrees. Without thinking I turned the dial to seventy. "Don't do that," Katia hissed, but didn't interfere. Seconds later we heard the furnace come to life. "Where can he be?" I asked. We weren't in a hurry to meet our grandfather. Now that we were inside the house and everything remained quiet, we took our time to look around. The dining room was a dark affair, with a table and six chairs but only one place mat. Here too, an empty cup of coffee had been left behind. The living room had plenty of windows and light, but the furniture looked as though nobody had used it in years. There were paintings of landscapes, some portraits, but no photos of the family, not even on the refrigerator. Opa had taken all of them down, none of the gold frames remained. A piano stood by the front window in the living room. Oma Anna had played, and Mom had received lessons until she was a teenager and stopped. The furniture, though old and unused, looked much nicer than our own. The room —and the whole house—appeared as though the plan for Opa's life had been much bigger than Mom and Dad's.

"We should have moved in here," I said. "Opa Frank doesn't need all that space."

"You're a monster," my sister said. "He worked hard for this."

"But it doesn't feel as though he lives here much." The old television set had been moved into a corner, and a giant over-stuffed leather armchair had been pushed in front of it. It made me realize how long we hadn't set foot in Opa's house. "Look, it's electric," I said. "You can move the backrest." Two pillows and a folded blanket lay on the chair, tidy, waiting for their owner's return.

"Is anybody here?" Katia shouted.

Beyond the staircase was a hallway with Opa Frank's office or library to the left and a small bathroom at the end. The office contained a desk and four large bookcases, and the blinds were drawn. The bathroom contained next to nothing, just a bar of soap and a towel. Lid and seat were still lifted; Katia screwed up her face.

We stood at the bottom of the stairs for quite some time, shouting the old man's name twice more. The downstairs of a house was, we even understood back then, for show, kept in a somewhat acceptable state because a neighbor might stop by, or you had to open the door for the mailman, the girl scouts, the neighbor who had lost his cat. The downstairs belonged to everyone—you ate or watched TV together, you had friends over for dinner or drinks—but the upstairs was private. You couldn't be sure of what you might find. I hadn't climbed the stairs since Oma Anna's death.

But of course, we weren't about to leave without having checked every room. We knew we wouldn't make our way home without at least having tried to find our grandfather. Maybe he could hear us and was not able to respond. Maybe he needed our help. "You go first," Katia said at last.

I pretended it was no big deal, tried to quieten my breathing. I expected Opa to appear at the top of the stairs and ask sharply what in the world we were doing in his house. The steps were uncovered, the wood groaned. I was reluctant to release my grip on the bannister. The distance between me and my sister increased, yet the noise I made didn't receive an answer. No one heard me approach, no head appeared in front of me as I climbed up the last step. There was only more silence.

"Which one is his bedroom?" I said.

Katia shrugged. Soon she joined me, her hand finding mine and squeezing it. "Don't you think it's weird that there are no pictures of Mom or of us in the house?"

The question startled me. "We can talk about that later," I whispered. "Opa Frank?"

·

You don't have to sleep to see nightmares. As a young kid, I cried when Opa picked me up or if I was left alone with him. That's what I was told. As a teenager, I noticed that my hands were his hands, only larger already at fourteen. My jaw was his, my narrow face as well. I didn't look much like Dad; my Mom left me with her cheeks and something about the eyes that seems obvious only when I turn my head to the left.

My earliest memory of Opa Frank is from the time my dad still drove his small red coupe, and Katia and I still fit in the backseat without banging our heads against the low ceiling. Dad had met Mom while he was in the military and she attended college down south. Katia was born while he was deployed, and a year before his discharge, Mom was expecting again. After buying and losing a restaurant, they decided they wanted to raise their kids in Mom's hometown. Opa Frank had offered to help them buy a house, and it turned out to be the one right next to his.

On the day we moved, Mom and Dad were driving the rental truck. Because Mom didn't have a license yet and couldn't drive us herself, Opa Frank drove Dad's car with Katia and me in the backseat. He was a heavy smoker. I remember the blue cloud spreading inside our car, and I felt safe. I neither liked nor disliked the man—I hardly knew him. Yet I felt safe because he didn't seem to concentrate the way Dad did, who gripped the steering wheel hard and shushed us whenever Katia or I asked a question. Opa Frank didn't care about us, he just did what needed to be done. I looked out at the cars we passed and those who passed us, and the hum of the engine made me wish we'd never arrive. No, I didn't love Opa Frank, but he was like some pungent new food you try—you spit it out that first time already knowing you'll try it again later.

We had lived outside of town down south, away from lights and stores and bars. I don't remember much of Ann Arbor, only an old lady peeling a tangerine for me and a view of our muddy backyard. I had no images, nothing to prepare me for where we were going. Maybe I fell asleep in the car on our way up north, but I was awake when we entered the small town after dark on a day at the end of November, and I leaned my head against the window. The lights of oncoming cars, of the storefronts, the streetlights along Main Street, seemed so very bright. They held a promise of new things to come, and even though I didn't move in my seat, I was wildly excited, sweaty in my winter coat. Was the heat broken? Was Opa Frank concerned we'd catch a cold when he rolled down the window to let the smoke escape? Whatever the reason, I wore my coat inside the car and felt the sweat on my skin and forehead. I was taking in the lights of this small town as though I had arrived in a vast metropolis. For the first time that day, Opa Frank told me to be quiet.

The moving truck already filled the driveway, furniture spilling forth onto the lawn and porch. Mom and Dad came to the car and picked us off the back seat. The house was brightly lit, and I begged to be set down. I wanted to see it all, climb the stairs, look at the rooms. I was hungry, thirsty, and I wanted to see all there was to see. Yet Mom and Dad carried Katia and me into a bedroom on the first floor, undressed us, and told us to go to sleep. Soon darkness bore down on us, and all the noises from moving boxes and furniture lost their excitement and turned menacing. The noises were outsized and shapeless. I lay in a wooden bed with bars in front of my eyes. My arms reached through those bars and found nothing.

·

When I was almost six, my grandmother died of cancer. Mom said that Opa Frank never forgave himself for not saving his wife. He was a doctor and should have known the lump near her neck wasn't benign. He should have sent her to a specialist immediately. He'd thought too much of himself and his abilities. He was a small-town doctor. He was a pediatrician in an area that time had only grazed.

After the funeral, we learned that we hadn't lost one grandparent, we had lost two. Instead of candy and quarters, Katia and I received warnings from Mom not to disturb Opa's peace. He stopped inviting us into his house. "I'm no cook," he said and stopped for dinner at Anthony's or made himself a sandwich at home. He gave up smoking from one day to the next and never talked about it again, almost as though he'd completely forgotten.

I left for school before Opa left his house next to ours. Around half past six in the evening, after having seen his last patient, he might appear on our porch, knock on the door and refuse to come in. "Just wanted to say hello," was a standard phrase. "Don't want to miss the news." He might stand outside on the porch and talk to Mom, but he rarely ate with us. Days he worked in his office on Main Street, and Mom worked the reception desk for a year before she received the same job at Dr. Koren's practice.

Even in his own house he disappeared for long stretches of time. Mom told us that before she left for college and before her own mother had died, Opa Frank spent the weekends in the basement, in what he called his museum. As a young man, he had travelled by train all over Europe and Asia, and his photos of train engines from around the world covered most walls. On index cards, he had typed the year and location and engine number. Often he was in the pictures as well; his friend Olaf had taken them. Olaf had been his companion on most trips abroad.

Anna had not shared Frank's obsession with trains and foreign cultures. She didn't like to travel, instead preferred to stay home and work in the garden. She wanted to have seven children, Mom told us, but endured a hysterectomy after Uncle Bobby was born. He was the youngest, Aunt Maggie the oldest. Bobby now lived in Minnesota, where he owned a car repair shop. Maggie had run away with a construction worker the day she graduated from high school. Only Mom had fulfilled the expectations of her dad and gone to college. But as a junior majoring in art history, she'd met Dad and soon become pregnant. "We're all colossal disappointments to him," she said. "He wanted one of us to take over his practice. He wanted one of us to be a doctor and talk doctor things with him. None of us kids were even any good in biology. Dad wanted someone who could talk shop with him, someone he could respect. He hated Koren and how handsome he was. He called him Dr. Television."

"Why didn't he move away?" Katia asked.

"It's not easy to start a practice and hold on to your patients. And this town is where your Oma was from. She liked it here. So he made his peace with the situation. And he let us know every day of the week that he made his peace with us kids. When Mom lamented that she couldn't bear more children, he'd scoff and say, 'What do you need any more for? Look at how badly we failed with these three. Why would we keep going?' He laughed every time he said that and he meant every word."

Maggie had been his favorite. After she ran off, he never talked about her again, as though she'd been a bad habit like smoking. At odd times, as if in thought, he'd start, "If Maggie were..." and then catch himself and fall silent. "I was the second, the least interesting child. But after she left, he sat down with me every night to help me with my homework. He insisted on it. He said I needed to get my grades up so I'd be accepted to a good college. Every day after dinner, after Mom had cleared the table, I had to show him my homework and he would go over it. I should have loved his attention but I hated every minute of it. I didn't want to be Maggie's replacement. Once I told him so, and he slapped my face. Bobby escaped his attention, I don't know how. He smoked weed, drank, and drove around in souped-up cars with his buddies. Dad never complained about him. I guess he saw him as a lost cause."

•

Opa hadn't died in his bedroom, nor did he lie slumped in the bathroom. The bathtub remained empty. We opened the door to the room Mom and our aunt had once shared, and we inspected Uncle Bobby's room, which Oma Anna had turned into a quilting room. Opa Frank had left it untouched. Boxes with colorful material were still stacked in the closet, and several unfinished projects lay folded on the small bed.

"Where can he be?" Katia asked. "Did he leave town before the storm and forget to tell us?"

"But he wouldn't have forgotten to lock the backdoor," I said.

She shrugged. "Maybe he did." Something relaxed in her face. An empty house might have seemed better to her than finding our Opa sick or dying. Better maybe than finding him in good health. Our steps forgot to be hesitant, our voices grew louder. We walked back into Opa Frank's bedroom, one side of the bed without pillow or comforter. I pulled open the top drawer of his dresser. A gold watch lay among small boxes with keys, pens, batteries, and light bulbs. I picked it up; the Rolex seemed very old and was small, too small for even my wrist, I thought.

"Put that back," Katia said.

I stuck out my tongue and instead put the watch around my wrist. Without her comment I wouldn't have done that, but now she couldn't persuade me to return it to its place. "It's mine," I said.

"You can't steal it," she said.

"He's not here."

Together we went down the stairs and inspected living room, dining room, office and bathroom a second time. There was nobody in the house. Only when we were already at the backdoor once again, did we remember. Of course we knew where Opa Frank was. He had to be in the basement. He had to be in his museum.

It felt odd not to have thought of this before, but then, neither Katia nor I had visited Opa Frank in years. As a small boy, all the photos of trains and various hats and signs had fascinated me, but I had become interested in girls, and girls and trains didn't mix. A kiss was worth more than a million miles of train tracks.

The door was one in a row of three in the narrow hallway separating the entrance area from the kitchen; the other two housed linen closet and furnace. You could overlook the third easily, and once I opened it, the dank basement smell made me scrunch up my face. "Opa Frank?" I shouted, then remembered the wristwatch, took it off, scooted into the kitchen, and left it on the counter right next to the dirty coffee mug.

"And if he's dead?" Katia's whisper brushed my ear as soon as I had taken the first step down. She slung her arms around me, held me back. And I stood silent, didn't move. "We should look for a flashlight," she said. But seconds later we found a light switch, and suddenly the basement didn't appear so dank anymore. The stairwell was wood-paneled, and the light fixtures stylish, if old. The stairs were covered in carpet.

"Opa Frank?" I shouted yet again. We received no answer.

The museum appeared largely unchanged, though I couldn't be certain. The walls were still covered in black-and-white and faded early color photographs. The space was large, maybe three-quarters of the house's footprint, and even though it felt damp now, the space was well-maintained. It seemed to have received upgrades—here, too, the walls were wood-paneled now, and the lights were no longer naked bulbs. If there had been any windows, the space might have been called friendly. Opa Frank was nowhere to be seen.

"The shed is the only other place where he could be," Katia said. The structure in back was quite large and housed garden tools and old furniture.

"No way," I said. "There's too much snow. And we would have seen his tracks. At least we tried," I added.

"Yes, we tried." Katia said in a low voice. "I don't get it."

"He was abducted by aliens. Or by the CIA. He's in the attic, hiding from the cops."

"You're a stupid potato face." Katia's voice betrayed her, she was as relieved as I was that we hadn't found our grandfather's corpse. "I'll leave a note saying we're looking for him."

•

The car appeared after I had cleaned the dishes the following night. The storm abated, and new snow was falling, light and silvery like stardust. Katia was playing music on the record player, something that sounded like bearded men strumming brittle guitars and singing with a stone lodged in their throats. You could hear the exhaust note of the car beyond the music. It was a deep burble, the dream of every boy and man in town. Then the noise stopped. Moments later, our doorbell rang.

Katia was wearing dad's fishtail parka over a long t-shirt that had belonged to her boyfriend and was ten sizes too big for her. "You go," she whispered.

I tried to wrench open the door, then shouted, "Just a minute," and got hot water from the kitchen. The man on the porch was laughing by the time I appeared in the frame. "Sorry to bother you," he said in a deep voice. He had black and gray stubble covering the lower half of his face, curly gray and black hair, and he wore a sheepskin coat, jeans, and cowboy boots. His hands were thick and raw. "I've been trying to get in touch with your neighbor. Any chance you know where I might find him?"

In front of Opa's house, an old Pontiac stood parked. It was a large beast, white with blue racing stripes. Because of the snow, the car stuck halfway out onto the street. It had seen better days.

What I did next I had been trained not to do, but something about this man told me he wasn't out to hurt Katia or kill us. Maybe I didn't care if he did. "You want to come in?" I asked. Behind me, the music stopped.

"No-o-o," I heard my sister from the living-room, and the man must have heard her too because he asked, "You sure it's okay?"

"Yeah," I said, blushing. "Come on in." I already wanted him to like me.

Katia had buttoned up the parka when we entered the house. She looked furious and scared, if that mixture is possible to show on a face at once. Or maybe her expression changed depending on who she looked at. "Hi," she said, her cheeks and neck deep red. Dad had never told us if he had killed anybody during the war; that secret made wearing the parka special.

"I'm really sorry." The man wasn't tall but burly. Something about him felt violent, maybe he slept in his car most nights. He wore a gold stud in one ear, and a gold necklace was visible before it sank into black hair and past the collar of his flannel. On his wrist he wore a big watch with a blue and red bezel. "You guys alone?"

"No," Katia said, "Mom and Dad are just running some errands. They'll be right back."

"Good," the man said. "Listen, I don't want to keep you…"

"You want some water?" I asked.

The guy laughed. "Sure, water would be great. Listen, I haven't been in this town in a long time. I tried calling your neighbor, but he always hangs up on me. I sent him a letter, and he never responded. I don't know, but is the Holmstrom family still living there? Or have I been bothering a perfect stranger?"

"Opa is still living there," I said. Water was leaking from

the man's boots onto the floor. I must have stared, because he looked down and apologized.

"Just water." He took out a handkerchief and crouched.

"Wait." I grabbed a dish towel and put it down in front of him. "That'll do."

Politely, he stepped onto the towel. "So, you guys know him?"

"He's our grandfather." Katia kneeled on the sofa, the parka hiding her completely. Only her head, ankles, and feet were visible.

"No shit," he said. "And your mom is…?" He was out of breath, couldn't finish the sentence. A button on his shirt was missing.

"Why do you want to know?"

"I might be an old friend of your mom's."

"Why are you here?" Katia's voice was high and brittle.

The guy raised his hands, open-palmed. "I'm really sorry. You don't know me. I should have introduced myself. I'm Paul."

"Paul who?" she asked.

"Paul Deming. I knew your mom when she was a teenager. We were…" Again, he seemed out of breath, shook his head at the sound of his hoarse voice. "When do you think she'll be back?"

"Soon," Katia said. "Do you know Dad as well?"

The man bit his lip. A crooked, sad smile pulled at his face; it might not have been a smile at all. "No, no I don't know him. And I didn't know that…I had thought that maybe…that maybe she hadn't married at all."

"Why wouldn't she have married?" I asked.

"Because he was her boyfriend," Katia said. "Oh my god."

"I'm really sorry," the man who'd told us his name was Paul said. "If I'd known she lived next door. I didn't have her number. I shouldn't have come like this. She was…Maggie and I were close back then."

Katia's face turned from him to me. Her eyes looked as though she would never blink again. I shrugged my shoulders, but she kept staring at me until I said, "Aunt Maggie doesn't live here anymore."

"Our Mom's Carol, her younger sister," Katia said. "You should really go now."

The man's face relaxed, his cheeks falling, his mouth standing open. He looked very stupid there and then. Stupid and old and dirty. But he didn't notice his open mouth, he was all by himself in his head. "Do you know where Maggie lives?" he said at last. "I've asked that old crank a hundred times, but he's not answering at all."

"She ran away with some guy," I said. "A long time ago, right after graduation. Some construction worker. They were trying to build a convention center here in town."

The guy didn't move, not for a long time. I'd never given him the water I'd offered, so I finally opened the cupboard, reached for a glass, and poured some. He took it without looking my way, without thanking me. When he spoke, his voice was unsteady. "And where's your grandfather now?"

I shrugged. "We haven't seen him in days. What kind of watch is that?" I pointed at his wrist.

It took him a second to understand the question. "A Seiko," he said. "A Japanese watch."

"Why is it blue and red?"

"It's a dive watch. It's called a Pepsi bezel." He undid the wristband and handed the watch to me. "Do you mind if I wait for your mom and dad? I'd love to ask them some questions. Will only take a few minutes."

"Katia lied," I said while inspecting the watch. It was heavy and chunky, not pretty when you looked more carefully; I wanted it badly. "Our parents are in Africa right now building a church and a school. They won't be back for months, maybe longer. And Opa Frank hates Maggie for running off and won't talk about her."

My sister got up from the couch. She was furious—I could tell without even looking at her, but I also sensed something more specific and delicate. "Are you hungry? I could make spaghetti," she asked Paul. In her bare feet, the parka drooping from her shoulders, she walked up to him, took the empty glass and put a hand on his arm, as if to reassure him everything would be okay. I don't know if she had decided that Paul was harmless, or if she wanted to show me that she wasn't afraid. Was she angry enough at me to be reckless?

"Another time," Paul said. "Thank you, that's very kind. If you see your grandfather, could you please let him know that I'm trying to reach him? I'm staying at the Great Lakes Motel. I'd be very grateful if he could spare the time."

"We'll tell him," Katia said. "If we see him. Feel free to stop by tomorrow. I can make dinner, I know how to cook."

"Thank you." Paul still seemed shocked or just deeply disappointed to have made the trip in vain. "Yes, I might stop by tomorrow. Thank you for the water. You can also call the motel if your grandfather comes home. If that's okay."

"Our line is dead." I handed back the watch.

"Is that true? Well, then I'll see you tomorrow!"

It was Katia who saw him to the door, and together, pulling and prodding, they opened it in good time. She laughed when snow blew in her face and remained standing in the entrance until I heard the engine come to life. It didn't sound unlike Paul's voice. He gunned the engine several times, making Katia put her hands over her ears and smile. I stood and watched her, and I already knew that we wouldn't play dress-up that night and that she would turn off her lamp right away without reading or talking to me. The noise slowly faded, and at last Katia locked the door and came back into the kitchen. I expected to be scolded, but she hardly noticed my presence. "Huh," she said. "He seemed really nice."

2

By chance I have been spared. If my luck doesn't hold, I am lost. I have wished to fall in step with my peers, be as well-worn and invisible as they are, visible only when asked. I envy people who enter the store and pick exactly, without thought or fail, the items the whole town has picked before them. Call it conformity, but I don't. Knowing what's best for you, your purchase will cause you no pain. Your loved ones won't worry about you, agree with you instead. They care about the Detroit Lions, though they'll never win a championship; they buy the brand everybody favors these days, in the style friends and colleagues favor right now; and they know without putting it into words that this buys them impunity. Even outsiders like Ed Glasgow, the town menace and owner of a rusty old Chevy truck with hand-painted flames on its sides, a guy whose flannels and jeans were dirty and whose hair was unkempt, and who lived alone in his dead mother's house out on Mackinac Lane and was the last person who saw Linda Brand alive before she disappeared, even Ed Glasgow served a purpose. He made everyone grateful for their own bland choices—and if you were good, you'd soon be like them.

I'm not enough to scare people off at first glance, I'm no Glasgow, but once I open my mouth, they recognize the small and ugly differences. They can detect absences. There isn't enough of me present, I won't belong. My paintings make people uncomfortable. I never paint but one woman, in a style that, though undoubtedly curious and particular, has not evolved. At times art magazines remember me and come calling. The internet is the graveyard of those that once showed promise. When sales flag, I pick up classes at one of the local colleges, but for the most part sales are steady. I have my admirers and I don't know who they are. If I were ever invited into their houses, I imagine these to be repugnant spaces, full of awful acquisitions and of poor taste.

I grew up in this small town. I lived my small-town coming-of-age tale, one the basics of which most of us share. I should be familiar to you. I should admit to my mistakes and say that I redeemed myself later on. We are all in love with ourselves, are we not? We spin events that mean little into stories of obstacles overcome, challenges met, and use the words that at some point held meaning but now only signal to an imagined audience that we indeed have a story. In my case, a story in which I turn from victim to villain to hero, from young and wild to a bit older and more measured. You want to share in my story because you hope it will be your own. But my small-town story doesn't end your way. No one likeable emerges. Redemption is a lie.

An artless word is foolish, a smooth forehead points to insensitivity, but I don't have the language you'd prefer. I don't recognize cause and effect—like redemption, it's a lie people tell each other to feel better about the world and their part in it. Cause and effect are like God and Devil; they are stand-ins for something more and less complex, creating a story about the story we're going to tell. Cause and effect—the man in the moon and the stork who delivers babies. If your mind is coarse and in need of stability, cause and effect might work wonders.

We don't know where and how eels mate.

Much only accumulates, like so much dirt after you dig a hole in your backyard. I have nightmares of living again in that house in our small town, my parents still living there together as though life had never occurred. I am reduced to my teenage self, mute with horror, swatting at affection that's forced upon me. "We love you," the ghosts say and cling.

I don't have a story. I have moments, and I'm afraid you will not find them to your liking. There's little to like, and I might not have the language to wrap my moments adequately for you. I should be near the completion of my life and be able to string events together as though they belonged in a certain order and revealed a meaningful pattern. I look back, and there's still only a construction site. The plan can't be gleaned from what's visible, there are only half-framed rooms that someone has worked on but never finished. The yard is unkempt. Weeds have claimed everything that is not made of stone, and those stones are barely visible under the careless growth of greedy plants I can't name. You see the past of this never-finished site, but there's no story.

That doesn't mean nothing happened.

The things I say turn people silent. I am not what you want to hear, I am not the person you want to hear it from. You want to learn, you want to relate and empathize, and I only have my life to give you. What happened and what I did will make you despise me. Maybe, or maybe you'll keep reading because you like watching things you feel could never happen to you, could never tempt you. This is my fear—that the way I have to tell what happened, the only way I can tell it, will mute everything. Maybe telling you about my life will untell it, make you turn your head the way you do when passing a homeless encampment on your way to the dentist. Maybe you can't see me and won't ever see me because what you see fills you with dread. I speak, and the words don't reach you.

She was never there. I'm lost.

Let me try again.

•

In the fall after I turned eighteen, a wildfire destroyed a large logging area to the west but stopped short of our town. For days, we saw dark clouds drift overhead, our noses and lungs stung. By then, I was dating Rebecca Karvonen. I was taller than either Mom or Dad and made the football team as a wide receiver. On Fridays after dark, I was afraid to lose sight of the ball in the stadium lights, afraid it would slip through my hands and hit me in the face. I hated getting hit while going after the ball and missing my target. I dropped the ball numerous times, yet I was speedy. I was gangly and could outrace anyone on the field. The ache in my chest whenever I sprinted toward the end zone on an overthrown pass I might just reach in time made me happy. Practice I often skipped citing brittle ankles.

Katia had found work at the local hardware store and took classes at the community college the next town over. I didn't want to let her see me weak. I was the wide receiver in a gold and scarlet uniform. We were the Miners, and I was popular with girls. Julie, a cheerleader with long brown hair and fresh-ly-removed braces, asked if I had a car. Dad drove a Chevy truck and Mom a Vega. She loved that car, bad rep and all, and had nursed it back from the dead twice already. Borrowing either of the two proved impossible. Julie sighed; not owning a car was worse than dirty underwear, worse than pimples and ingrown toenails. My friend Miles, who lived alone with his mom in an old house on Bay City Avenue, said I should forget about her. "She has a boyfriend, and, I don't know, but I have the feeling she'll die in this town."

"She's seventeen. She's not going to die."

Miles rolled his eyes. "What I mean is, she'll never leave town. If you hook up with her, you'll be chained to this town forever."

Rebecca said I was immature and cute. She said that with-out prompt one day in the cafeteria, after I had agreed to meet Julie at Fancy's later that afternoon. "You don't even like her." Becca was repeating her senior year and barely received pass-ing grades. She had red hair, red skin, and large hands and feet. After making that remark, she walked off, her bag slung over her shoulder. Her old shiny leather coat was the kind that looked as though you were carrying a million dollars in small bills in your bag. I followed her into the school library.

"No one can ever see us together," she said after our first kiss in the stacks. "I'd rather die than be seen with you." She taught me to bite her lip until it bled, and to pinch and pull her nipples as though I wanted to hurt her. "It's gross," she said. "I'm gross. But you're lucky to have me, I guess." Her skin was dry, rough, bristly. She smelled salty, she burnt my tongue.

•

By September, Mom's palm trees had died. The peach and man-darin-orange trees had lost their leaves and the small branches broke easily. The only plant that survived was a fir Dad had bought in anticipation of Christmas time. Mom's cacti were rotted, her butterfly tree only stood upright because she had wired it to a fence post.

After coming home from Indonesia, Dad had landed a job at the mine, but Dr. Koren had a new receptionist and no need for a second employee at that position. We'd be okay, Dad said, and Mom didn't answer and wouldn't look at him. Her see-saw smile lasted us all night.

For some time, she stocked shelves after closing at the hard-ware store where Katia was working at the checkout, but she left abruptly without ever saying why. They'd been gone for three years and as soon as they returned to our small town, she started to plant trees. She now wore sandals all year round and after the first snow, she wore them with rough gray socks. Her face was wide, her hair curly. Her voice could cut through glass.

Mom loved Reagan and was suspicious of Nancy. She thought her haughty but never missed any of his speeches. Whenever Mom switched on the TV to watch the president, Dad quietly left the room to smoke a cigarette on the porch or sit on a lawn chair in the snow out back. From my room, I could see the glow of his cigarette at night, and beyond our yard the even darker expanse of Siberia. Our property ended by the railroad line that connected the mine with the harbor some twenty miles away. Dad was a quiet man and had grown even quieter. You could prod and poke him, and he would not lose his calm. He was bearded now, maybe making up for his nearly bald head or for the loose skin on his neck. He asked about school, about what I thought about going to college, about joining the military, about getting a car. People didn't move to our town to build a future; they came after they'd run out of choices. But Mom and Dad, after spending three years away, still owned the house right next to Opa Frank's. They could afford the life they hadn't been able to buy elsewhere. Dad's bald pate was wet with perspiration.

He and Mom had come back for us, they said, but Katia and I felt that this was only partially true. We had survived three years without them—the children they'd left behind no longer existed. Now our parents expected to pick up where they had left off. They rearranged the furniture; they put their toiletries up in Katia's bathroom. Mom took down Katia's cartoons and hung photos of herself in groups of Senegalese children, in groups of Indonesian children. I asked Dad, "What kind of cars did you drive?"

"I didn't drive," he said. "Not much anyway. There was no need to drive."

"What did you do for fun?"

He took off his glasses, pushed them onto his nose again. "We had fun," he said. "We had our fun."

Katia and I inspected Mom's photos when she wasn't around but couldn't recognize the person living with us. Our parents had turned into remembered relatives from distant family reunions, friendly strangers we didn't quite understand or wished to share our home with. They were no closer to us than our teachers, only that they owned our place. Thus, my old room that for three years had served only as storage, was 'my room' again. I spent as little time as possible there.

Katia's boyfriend Scott rented a trailer out on a dirt road, and she only stayed at home when he was away. Scott was a burly guy who played the guitar and worked on freight ships crossing Lake Superior. They had two cats, Angry and Furious, and sometimes, when I stayed out with Rebecca until late, I slept on their couch instead of going home.

•

After making out, Rebecca would pull books from the shelves and show me. Always the same books. They were coffee table books of New York, with street scenes and skyscrapers and apartments looking out on Central Park. Becca had cut her own figure from family photographs and put it on top of the Chrysler building and in front of a barber shop on Amsterdam Avenue. "I was meant for New York," she said. "I didn't fail senior year, if you want to know."

"Then why are you repeating it?" I asked.

"They made a mistake. Miscalculated my scores. But when they found out it was too late."

"Your parents couldn't fix that?" The Karvonens had owned the Great Lakes Motel for generations and lived on Grant Street, the most expensive one in town. They were veritable bluebloods.

Rebecca shook her head. "Somehow I think this town doesn't want to let me go. It's the town's fault, for sure. Now I have you to prove it."

I decided not to think about that last remark, not to scrunch up my face. "What will you do?" I asked. "In New York?"

She shrugged. "Anything."

"Broadway?"

"Fuck Broadway," she said. "I'll get lost, I'll get sucked into the city. I'll speak all the languages of the world. People will walk all over me."

I laughed at that last line. Her fist broke my nose.

•

Sunday afternoons belonged to my visits with Opa Frank. He no longer worked Fridays, only went to his practice Monday through Thursday. "I'm getting too old for a full schedule," he said. On Saturdays, he occasionally put an easel in the trunk of his Lincoln and left town to paint the coast, the lake, the harbor. Watercolors and pencil drawings took up the space photos of our family had occupied while Oma Anna had been alive.

Sunday mornings, Opa went to church, but in the afternoon, he'd take me out for ice-cream or early dinner and talk about his childhood, how he had worked to put himself through medical school and traveled the world. I wasn't much interested in his stories but I was interested in him being interested in me.

I remember driving to Marquette with him. He took me to a diner, and after the waitress had placed the food in front of us, he said, "Your parents lack vision. They act impulsively. But you need more than that to get through life."

"Why do I have to 'get through' life?" I asked. "It's not some jungle or drought or war."

"It's worse," he said. "What keeps mankind alive? The fact that millions are daily tortured, stifled, punished, and silenced. Mankind can keep alive thanks to keeping its humanity repressed."

In response, I looked down at my burger, picked off the onions, scraped off the mayonnaise.

He continued, "Your grandmother died, but I wasn't finished with her."

"Not finished?"

"I'm not senile. I needed a partner."

I thought about this, but the blurry images I conjured repulsed me. "Why didn't you remarry?"

"Ours is a small town. Where do you find the right one?"

I thought of Rebecca, who I knew didn't think of me as the right one. I shook my head. Speaking with Opa Frank about love made my burger and shake taste funny. The colors were off, too. At the same time, I wanted him to ask more questions, to tell me more about my parents. "Are Mom and Dad the right ones for each other?"

"You tell me." He waited for my response.

"Even when they're both home they're never in the same room."

Opa Frank nodded. "She's planting a lot of trees now."

"So why don't you have lunch with *her*?"

He looked at me until I lowered my eyes again and took another bite of my food. "I never had any feelings for her. There was no connection. She wasn't a bad child; she was better behaved than the other two, and she is the one who stayed. I should be thankful for that. And I am. I do appreciate that she returned to this town and is trying to make a life here. But I look at her, and there is, you know, nothing. If she left again tomorrow for Korea or Vietnam, I would hardly notice."

"And Dad?"

"He's a decent man but a fool. You can't be Mormon and believe in science at the same time. You are either betraying your religion or yourself. Look at the Book of Mormon—it's full of verifiable lies. There's not a crumb of truth in any of these pages. So how can you respect yourself and spread those lies?" He finished his own burger and fries. His tongue swished around in his mouth searching for pieces of meat lodged in his long teeth. "I admire happy fools. You see, if something stupid gives you deep satisfaction—go for it. If you believe lies to be true and they make you happy—fine. But your dad is not fulfilled. You can smell it on him."

"Because he drinks and smokes?"

Opa's jaw tightened, his lips thinned. "You're talking symptoms. He's lost his way. He's lost."

"What should I do after high school?" I asked.

"What do you want to do?"

"I'm not sure," I answered truthfully. "I might get a football scholarship. Coach says he's talked to recruiters. I could go to college."

"But you don't want to?"

I thought about my answer. If I were ever to get any real advice from anybody, it was Opa Frank, because he kept to himself and didn't care. "I want to go to New York. But whenever I try to imagine it, whenever I try to imagine going to a good school or working at a good job, I'm not in the picture. I can either imagine the city or myself, but never together."

He stood up, left a few bills on the table, and walked toward the exit. I hurried after him. "What do you think?"

"You've answered your own question. In this world, you

must make your own bed. No one will show you how. You can lie down and get kicked if you want to. As for me, I would rather stand and kick."

We were silent on our drive home, and I tried not to look his way, kept my eyes on the side of the road. We didn't speak again for two weeks.

•

"How are your folks?" Ed Glasgow asked one night sitting on the tailgate of his old Chevy. Most every night, you could find him in the parking lot of Fancy's. Not many people stopped to talk to him; he had the kind of reputation that prevented someone like dad from ever sharing a beer with him—and he always bought beer at Fancy's, plenty of it, and if he was in the mood he shared. A year earlier, Linda Brand, a deaf student, had vanished after he had offered her a ride. The girl had never been found, even though Sheriff Gautier had searched Ed's house on Mackinac Lane and the woods behind it. The town was divided over who was to blame for Linda's disappearance. Grant Street, where our town's old money lived, firmly believed in Ed's guilt, whereas Dogwood, an area of cheap tract homes and rusted cars, blamed the parents for not having taught their daughter properly. The Brands' marriage hadn't survived Linda's assumed death. Only her mother Karen still lived in town. While Ed's visibility hadn't suffered, Karen Brand was rarely seen, mostly after hours. She was a shadow, she didn't buy at Fancy's.

Ed called me Shithead and shared beers with me. It was an okay trade, beer for the occasional insult. That night I was in a mellow mood; Julie and I had bought ice-cream, then spent time in the trees beyond the dumpster. I felt generous with my time and attention. My shirt was full of dirt and needles.

"They seem lost," I said.

"And your sister?" He didn't even look at me, just watched the smoke getting away from him.

"What about her?"

"I see her running around with Scott Hurme. She's hot. Legs up to here."

"Don't talk about her. She's not some girl you can pick up. You're gross."

"Watch it, Shithead." His voice was deeper now, quieter, and I was afraid of him then, unable to move or breathe. "She's too good for you," he continued. "A bit on the boring side, but too good for this town. She'll run away like your aunt, just to get the fuck out of this place."

"Did you know my aunt?" I coughed midway through my question, my mouth dry.

"A little. She was into older guys. I was only a junior when she graduated, doubt she ever realized I existed. Left the last day of school. Katia will leave too. I can feel it."

I swallowed, drank more beer to find something to say that didn't involve Katia. "I don't think my parents like it here anymore. Something happened while they were away, but they don't want to talk about it. Every time I come home it feels as though someone has died. It's that silent."

"Why did they come back?"

I shrugged.

"Exhausted men can't escape from here." He looked straight at me. "Behind every woman is a guy tired of fucking her. Maybe that's true the other way around too. Maybe your mom's doing something about that. Ever shot a gun?"

"No, no, that's…No."

"No fun imagining your mom enjoying sex, is it? My old lady enjoyed plenty of it after my dad left. Heard her all the time when I was young. Funny thing, she always sounded the same, no matter whose truck stood outside. Ever went out to hunt? Your dad is a vet, he probably killed a bunch."

I hastily finished my beer. I was afraid he would rip it from my hand if I answered. "Got to go," I said.

"Where you going? Can't get enough of Julie?"

"Don't say that."

"Mark won't be happy if he finds out. She's his girl. You're asking for trouble, Shithead."

"How do you even know?" I asked.

He handed me a second can. "I have eyes. You're not discreet. She isn't either. She's not as hot as your sister. Wonder why you'd settle after getting a taste of Katia."

I looked at the can, set it down, walked away. He laughed briefly in my back, but I'm certain he had forgotten about me long before I had vanished from sight.

That fall I often dreamed that I had learned to levitate. The first few times I had the dream, I panicked and was carried farther and higher into the clouds, knowing I would die if I ever fell back to earth. But later I managed to control how high I rose off the ground and started to explore our town at night, looking at all the people who were still out on the streets, and I sat in trees and watched them drink and smoke. I sat on the roofs of houses and could see what everyone below me was doing. Each time I had this dream I woke with my heart ready to burst and my chest hurting wildly.

·

Grant Street was our town's idea of grandeur—cars could have double-parked easily without slowing down traffic, and the houses were imposing Victorians, Colonials, Southern Plantation. The founding fathers of our town had lived here first, and their offspring still held on to most blocks.

The Karvonens' house was one of the smaller ones and yet was far more spacious than ours. Rebecca only let me visit when her parents had left and she and her grandma were alone in the house. Ingri was short, square, her hair thin, her hands full of liver spots. Her old Cadillac sat in the street in front of the house, all four tires flat, yet she wouldn't let anyone tow it away. Whenever Becca's father tried to have it moved, she would scream and curse, Becca said, as though she were possessed by a demon. I couldn't imagine Ingri intimidating anyone. Each time she saw me, she spread her arms and pulled me in to kiss my forehead. She said words that sounded ridiculous. I'd never heard them before; she smiled with yellow teeth.

Rebecca claimed that Ingri hadn't uttered a word of English in over ten years. She had spoken it fluently with a mere hint of an accent, but after her husband's death, she fell through what had once been safe netting. At first the pauses between words lengthened, as though she had to retrieve the right ones from some far-off corner. Then her old language reappeared. A word here and there. Words she had only spoken with her elders and not at all since their deaths. Her husband Ben had never learned a word of Finnish; his ancestors had gotten lost after setting foot in the New World and mixed with whomever they wanted or needed. There was no clear path back, nobody had left a trail of white pebbles, and the breadcrumbs had been picked off.

"At least one of us loves you." Rebecca concluded, locking the door to her room behind us. The Karvonens' motel was the only one in town, and sometimes Becca would work at the reception desk or clean. She never invited me to come over and steal into one of the many empty rooms. "Don't be a creep," she said when I suggested it. "That's totally inappropriate."

We could hear her grandmother walk up and down the creaky stairs, or she would knock on our door and ask something neither of us could understand. She was always around while I burrowed into Rebecca. Rebecca was quiet, hitting me with her palms and sometimes with her fists while I pinned her down the way she taught me. Later she jerked me off.

On days she wasn't working at the motel, Becca was in charge of bathing Ingri, and one week in early November, after we'd been in her room for hours, she said, "You can help me."

I said I couldn't. "It wouldn't feel right."

"She won't mind. She loves you," Becca said.

She put me in charge of the bathwater. A plastic thermometer in the shape of a dolphin read out the temperature. I called out to Becca when the tub was full, and she arrived a few moments later leading her grandmother by the hand. Ingri was wearing a pink terry-cloth robe, and after she'd entered the bathroom as though I weren't sitting on the edge of the tub, she opened the belt and let the robe fall to the ground. Holding on to the large silver handle, she climbed into the hot water. Then she turned and smiled at me and murmured something. She sounded pleased.

Becca left immediately, only saying, "The sponge is right there on the shelf."

I took it, dipped it into the foaming water and started to scrub the old woman's back. She kept muttering, which I took for a good sign. But a minute later Ingri sank back and closed her eyes, her breasts forming two islands. And I couldn't take my eyes off them; they were so full and white. I dipped the sponge again.

•

Miles had never gotten over Abba's break-up and was the only boy I knew still listening to the band. At least when we were alone; he was too smart to let anyone else know. He was shorter than me, had not kissed a girl yet. I was free to feel superior to him, and he let me read the notes he'd taken in class before every math and biology test. At thirteen, we'd played with his model trains all afternoon, but the tracks had long since disappeared. We studied together for exams in his bedroom, which Miles had recently adorned with guitars. If he was in an okay mood, he'd play in front of me. Miles was the lead guitarist for the Sturdy Turds. They rehearsed most weekends, and I wasn't allowed to join because I didn't play an instrument and couldn't sing either. Miles said they played Punk; they'd go to Detroit and make it big.

He owned a Minolta SLR camera his dad had given him for his birthday, and some Fridays he'd come and take pictures of the game. Mostly though, he drove out to the water, walked the beach, and photographed seagulls and waves and rocks, then developed the pictures in the basement, where his mother had set up a darkroom. He said he'd run into nudists in the summer.

I told him about Rebecca and Ingri, about Julie and Mark. "Who do you like better?" he asked. "Rebecca or Julie?"

I let myself think about that question, then shrugged. "Rebecca is older. It counts more, I guess."

"Do you like them, or do you like that they can't really be with you?"

I wasn't sure what he meant and told him so.

He adjusted his glasses with one finger; his nails were long now, always scrubbed. "Rebecca won't kiss you in public, and neither does Julie. Julie has a boyfriend, and Rebecca is waiting for someone better. You can't have either of them. Is that what excites you?"

I felt insulted, suspected jealousy. What did he know? "They love me," I insisted.

Miles nodded his head. "Yes, maybe. But they can't or won't be with you."

"So what?"

"You're some fun on the side. Nothing serious."

"That's much better," I argued. "They're with me because they want to, not because we're going to get married and have kids. It's a much better kind of love."

He looked up from his notebook, took off his glasses and wiped them with his shirt. "You're full of shit."

"And you're a virgin."

"If I stay a virgin, I'll never die."

"Seriously?"

"As long as you don't have sex, you're immortal. And you don't contract gonorrhea in the back of a car riding around county roads."

"I really need a car," I said.

"How are the trees?" Miles had seen the rows of dying plants, had seen my mom put new plants into the ground.

"They shouldn't have come back," I said. "It was much easier without them."

"Do you love them?"

"I feel like I should."

"But you don't."

"Katia moved out because they returned. Do you love your Mom?"

Miles looked intently at a page in his notebook, wouldn't meet my eyes. "If she left, I'd kill myself. Which is funny, because I can't stop thinking about getting out of this town. I want to leave so badly, but if she abandoned me, I'd go insane. I want to leave—I don't want to be left. It's pretty fucked up."

"But do you love her?"

"Yes, very much."

His answer was so quiet, we fell silent afterwards, as though we'd shared a dirty secret. At last, I said, "Glasgow said Katia's going to leave town."

"How does he know?"

I shrugged. "He says he can sense it."

"Bullshit. He is a sick fuck. Stay away from him."

I nodded. Katia couldn't leave. It was unthinkable. Into my silence, Miles grabbed one of his guitars, an old acoustic one full of stickers, and began playing something I didn't recognize, something he might have made up. I closed the math book and listened, and I wasn't in love with Rebecca or Julie any longer.

•

Two weeks before Thanksgiving I asked Mom if I could invite somebody over. New snow was falling on what was left of the old, and she stood with a shovel in the yard, her socks in sandals full of clumpy ice. "Miles is welcome anytime," she said.

"It's not Miles." That day, the mail had delivered boxes of new plants, and she had stacked them high. One by one, she cut them open and extracted geraniums, calla lilies, rosemary, and a lime tree. I stood watching her. Our coach had warned me I might be kicked off the team should I miss any more practices, and I had noticed I wasn't afraid of his threat. We had only won one game so far and had lost the last, against Marquette High, seventy-one to seven. But Rebecca had been in the stands watching me haul in our lone touchdown pass. Afterwards she'd said I looked like a god and given me a kiss in front of two- or three-hundred people in attendance, most of them from Marquette.

"Not Miles," Mom repeated. "Who is your girlfriend?"

"She's not my girlfriend."

"Oh my." She wiped her sweaty face, leaving claw marks of dirt on her forehead and cheeks. "She's the difficult type. Have you used a condom? I'm not old enough to raise any grandchildren."

"You're disgusting," I said.

She swung her shovel and hit me in the chest. "Watch your language. Help me with these trees."

•

The day before Thanksgiving, my dad came home around four in the afternoon. It was dark by then. His clothes were dirty; he hadn't showered or changed after work. Days at the mine were turning him silent, taking away most words. It seemed that he'd lost weight. Instead of having a drink in town, he hurried home to walk out into the backyard and past the fence into Siberia or smoke among Mom's dead trees. Sometimes when I hurried downstairs to grab something from the refrigerator, he sat by the window in the darkened living room.

That afternoon he got out of the truck and watched Mom in down coat, jeans, and sandals, plant a rosebush she'd acquired from a catalog. It had arrived heavily wrapped, but even so, the long journey to our town had nearly killed it. Leaves came off easily while Mom unwrapped it under the outside light above the kitchen door.

She'd heard the truck; its light had hit her in the back. She turned and said, "We're out of salt and butter, and I forgot to buy the cranberry sauce."

Dad nodded and kept standing by his truck, watching Mom bend down and straighten the rosebush and filling in the hole she'd dug. He watched her pour soil from a bag. "Let me take a shower first and afterwards I'll drive into town." The words sounded off, correct but not right, as though he were reading them from a dictionary. Then he walked up the stairs to the front porch, slipped out of his shoes and coat.

He took a long time getting ready. Dad wasn't too particular about his clothes, but he liked them clean. He liked them starched and stiff, he'd once explained to me, so he could feel how clean and fresh they were. The smell of aftershave found its way from our upstairs bathroom into the hall and the dining room and kitchen.

His hair was wet and slicked back when Dad reappeared downstairs wearing a blue button-down and black jeans. "Salt, butter, and cranberry sauce." Methodically he cleaned his glasses with a dish towel. "You and Katia need anything?" He grabbed his wool coat, took the keys from the phone table, stepped into his good boots, and left.

Around midnight, Mom called the police station and reported Dad as missing. She listened to the voice on the other end of the line, then said, "No," and "Not yet," and "I don't think so," and finally "Whatever you say."

She hung up, then rifled through the cabinets until she found an old, unopened bottle of wine and a half-full bottle of brandy they kept for guests and asked Katia and I if we wanted a glass as well. We sat around the coffee table, Katia and Mom on the leather sofa, me in one of the La-Z-Boys, our hands clinging to tumblers full of red liquid. She didn't talk, not a word. After her third glass she went into the bedroom.

Neither of us got dressed and into Mom's car to look for Dad's truck along the road into town. He could have wrapped the Chevy around a telephone pole, he could have slid into a ditch. We knew the odds.

•

More snow swept streets and yards that night and it never stopped snowing on Thanksgiving Day. Becca's Mom dropped her off at three that afternoon in a white Cadillac. Becca wore stockings, patent-leather dress shoes, and a thin black wool coat. Her long body was stuck in a satin dress; you could see the outline of her underwear. She had applied make-up, and as soon as I opened the door, I said, "Don't bring up my dad."

Mom was asleep on the couch, and we kept our voices down. The empty bottle of brandy and a bottle of pills stood on the coffee table. A down comforter covered her figure and face. From time to time I checked if the comforter was still moving with her breath.

Katia had pushed the turkey into the oven that morning, and together, the three of us started on the beans, the stuffing, the mashed potatoes. From time to time I put a hand on the small of Becca's back. Each time, she moved away and sucked in her breath.

Around five, long after all the windows had turned black, we switched off the overhead light, and Katia found two candles and three used tea lights and we put them on dessert plates and lit them. The turkey was overdone, so dry it was hard to swallow. The beans were already cold again, but stuffing and mashed potatoes, even without butter, much salt, or cranberry sauce, turned out fine. Mom was still asleep and at times made a whistling noise. She grunted repeatedly.

We sat at the kitchen table with the good china I had taken from the cabinet with the glass doors. Ever since Mom and Dad had returned from their mission, we had stopped using them. They felt light and brittle and their gold rims were discolored. Katia remembered Becca from a play they'd been in together, but the two had never met outside of school. Katia looked from Becca to me; her eyes were very large. "How did you guys meet?" she asked.

I had my mouth full, tried to squeeze an answer past the dry turkey but had to cough.

"I saw him eat turkey and thought he was cute," Becca said. "He's not a brainiac, though."

"I have other qualities," I wheezed.

Katia grunted. "He isn't all bad."

Becca lowered her voice from a whisper to a murmur. "So where is your dad? Is he in the hospital? Did he rob a bank? Did he cheat on your mom? Did someone bite his balls off?"

My mouth was already full again. I clamped a hand over it not to laugh.

Katia put down her fork. "Dad left us."

"Why?" Becca asked.

Katia shrugged. "They don't get along. Or maybe we were not enough. Or..." She paused for a moment, looked at her plate, then at the chandelier. "Maybe he couldn't watch all those plants die."

The ensuing silence turned the dining room sepia. I remembered Oma's stories of the Pity and how she and her crew had vanished into thin air. No body had ever been recovered. "Maybe he wanted new pussy." Even at the time I didn't know why I said that. It was the stupidest thing I could have said, yet I wanted to, I needed to. I desperately wanted to say it just to say it. I imagined Ed Glasgow sitting in his beat-up truck smoking a Camel. I imagined the Sheriff asking him about the deaf girl, asking to scour the premises.

Neither Katia nor Becca turned to look at me. They looked at the food on their plates, then at each other. Their forks scratched in unison. They took drinks of water at the same time.

"Maybe he has a girlfriend down south," I said, louder now. "Maybe he has two or three of them."

They should have told me to shut up. Becca should have taken my hand and pulled me close. I wish she had sealed my mouth with her red fingers which smelled of patchouli and cheap soap, soap she stole from the motel's supply for her personal use. I wanted to feel her fingers on my lips and be silent. Instead, she said, "I brought some pie. Katia, maybe we can heat it up." She pushed off her chair to look where she'd left the bag. Katia got up too to switch on the oven again. I looked at the rest of the stuffing; a seemingly drunk fly came out of nowhere, sat down on the rim of the bowl and scratched her legs.

Later we piled the dishes on the kitchen counter. Katia found my mother's old fur-lined coat for Becca, and a pair of my father's work boots that were only a little too big for her long feet. I gave her my beanie, and the three of us left the house and walked out into the backyard. With the moon on the shingles, we saw white on the snow. To the left stood Opa's shed, a big animal curled up, snow gathering on top and around it. Our faces were burning, my eyes watering, lashes freezing. At the far end, near the tree line, Katia paused and pulled something out of her coat pocket. "You guys want?"

I didn't know she was smoking weed, but after she'd taken a hit, Becca took the joint from her fingers, inhaled, coughed once, and passed it on to me. She stood in silence, peering up at a break in the clouds and the stars beyond. The snow was still falling, and dry, single crystals kept melting on our faces. I felt dizzy and I wanted nothing more than to sling my arms around Becca and open her coat and feel her bony body against mine. I wanted Katia to witness it, allow it, say it was all right.

"Let's walk through Siberia," Katia said.

Becca laughed. "Where is that?"

I pointed behind her.

"Let's go," she said.

The snow showed us the way through the blackness. Once the house had disappeared from view, no sound but the squeaking white existed. Katia jumped to pull at a tree branch and showered us with more snow. Our town, our home, school, and our parents, were hundreds of miles away.

"What are you guys going to do?" Becca was walking behind me, in front of Katia. "About your dad?"

Katia shrugged. "After spring, I'll be leaving."

"Where to?"

"Just leaving. You?"

Becca kept walking, didn't turn to us to answer. "I'll move to

New York. I know a guy there. He's a painter. He used to live here, rented a large space near the railyard. I really liked him. I can stay with him for a while."

I never slowed my steps, I was grateful for the darkness that hid my face. For me, New York had always existed by itself, an abstract idea with millions of people I didn't and wouldn't know. Pictures of the Flat Iron building and Grand Central. Becca had never told me about the painter. I had another seven months of school ahead of me and wouldn't even be able to visit.

"He is really very talented. He just signed on with a gallery," Becca added.

"I'd love to meet him," Katia said. "Have you been?"

Rebecca shook her head. "You're his type. If he asks you to sit for him, don't do it. You won't get out alive."

"You're alive," Katia said.

"He never asked me."

After twenty minutes, we reached the train tracks. We stood, turning this way and that, looking for bright headlights poking through the snow. Without a word, Katia stretched out across the ties, in-between the rails, and seconds later, Becca lay down on top of her, face turned toward the sky, and said, "Come." I lowered myself gently, slowly, the crown of my head coming to rest below Becca's chin. Snow started to cover my face. I couldn't keep my eyes open.

"So what really happened to your dad?" Becca said.

After a while, I heard Katia crying. I stared at the sky and I felt Katia's hands below me and I knew they were holding on to Becca. I lay perfectly still, wishing we could lie there forever, wishing too that I could run away from Katia, Becca, Mom, town, school, and the Miners. I didn't move, though. Not once did I move.

3

One Saturday afternoon in early December, after the wind had let up and the sun was pushing past long layers of clouds, Julie came over, and the silence in the house spooked us and we went out back to smoke instead. She said her boyfriend Mark was growing suspicious, he would hurt me should he ever find out she was at my place. He dealt weed, so she always had enough on her. We removed the snow from the garden furniture and sat, taking sips of water from time to time. Mom was running errands, and Opa Frank had gone painting down in Bay City. With every drag I grew more afraid my breath might stink. I didn't want to make out in the open, I didn't want to take Julie to my room where Mom might see her when she returned. Instead I suggested we try Opa Frank's old shed out back, near the tree line to Siberia. I'd been inside as a kid and knew where Opa hid the key. He stored old furniture inside, kept his garden tools there in the winter.

She didn't question my idea, which made me nervous. People usually refused to do whatever it was I suggested. I'd gotten used to the idea that something was off with me, that somehow I didn't pass muster. So when Julie listened to my suggestion and said, "Sure, let's go," I got up, baffled, and only mumbled, "Okay."

We trudged through the snow. There was no trail, there were no footprints; Thanksgiving night seemed weeks and weeks past. "If you patched it up and painted it and put in a small garden, you could live in there," she said.

"Yeah, it's big. I think at some point there were bats inside."

Julie scrunched up her face. "Are they still there?"

I shook my head. "Opa killed them, I believe."

The key was still on a hook under the ledge of the only window of the shed, to the right of the large double doors. I opened the padlock, put it in my coat pocket, and said, "Tadah!" looking at Julie's face while I pulled open the door. Her smile vanished, but not because of fear or disgust. It was something else, something bigger than her eyes; it gave me the chills. I turned away from her and followed her gaze. "Wow," she said slowly, "your Opa is fucking badass."

I didn't say anything for a long time. My head swirled. Smoking affected me in strange ways, cutting whole segments out of what I was doing, like cutting scenes from a movie and dropping them to the floor and out of sight. I still knew what I was doing, at least that's what I thought, but I couldn't be sure how I'd gotten to the point I found myself at. Too many actions and images were missing. "Shit."

"You've got to give me a ride," Julie said.

"Yes." We walked around the car, but the two doors were locked.

"Lock the shed." Julie took off her coat and pulled down her pants.

"Right here?" I asked after I had followed her command.

"Right here." She kissed me, and she didn't hit me or tell me to hit her. She took off one boot and one pant leg so I could enter her more easily, and she moved beneath me on the icy-cold hood of the old white Grand Prix with the blue racing stripes, pulled me close and held me, and her legs closed around me and didn't let go. My mind cut in and out, in and out, but the whole time I could hear Julie breathing and whispering my name. I didn't love her, not one bit.

•

Rebecca worked her parents' motel reception desk again before the holidays. A few engineers and managers and inspectors had driven north to pay the mine a visit. Becca was rarely busy but needed to be available. She didn't mind if I sat with her behind the desk. I helped her make fresh coffee to be put out in a big thermos on the lobby's credenza. The Great Lakes Motel had no kitchen, and breakfast consisted of packaged pastries and more coffee and powdered creamer. The light in the lobby gave everything a greenish-yellow hue; you couldn't fall in love with anyone you encountered.

"So you finally got laid," she said out of the blue one evening. Mom had relented and let me drive her Vega. It slid and skidded across the icy roads and turned every short trip into a nail biter.

"How do you know?" I looked up from an older issue of *People* magazine, in which singers and movie stars wore clothes that would have gotten them killed in our town.

"So she didn't lie?"

"Julie?"

"You're too easy," Becca said. "You wouldn't survive five minutes if the cops ever questioned you."

"Why would they?"

"Are you guys dating now?" Her voice was flat, giving me nothing.

"She has a boyfriend and he'll beat me up if he finds out."

"Huh," Rebecca said. "You sure about that?"

"Why would she lie?"

"To make herself more interesting?"

"But I am already interested. It doesn't make sense."

Rebecca only grunted. "I'm happy for you," she said after a while.

"Not jealous?"

"Of Julie?"

The way she said it—I thought about the answer without wanting to. It was much easier to be around Julie, and she seemed to genuinely care about me. We'd already done it in the football locker room and in a broom closet in school, right next to the biology lab. I had pressed my hand hard over her mouth so she wouldn't give us away. She was so *there*, there with me. "You should be," I said.

"Those large boobs? Ugh." She curled her upper lip, exposing slightly crooked front teeth.

"Katia has large boobs," I said.

"Large boobs?" We hadn't heard him coming down the stairs, and his sudden appearance startled us. The man wore a black coat, black jeans, and heavy boots. Maybe he was an inspector working for a few days at the mine; his nails were all clean. He laughed at our silence and open mouths. "But I'll settle for some food."

There were only two options if you didn't want a greasy burger from Sparcky's, our town's only bar. You could either go to Anthony's, the Italian place run by a former sailor who had settled permanently in the area, or you could try your luck at Fancy's, the convenience store who also operated a diner in back. "Sounds great," the man said after Rebecca had explained how to get to Anthony's. "I'll be ready for those large boobs after." He winked and stepped outside.

"Slime bag," I said.

"Yeah, really." Rebecca pulled open a drawer, took a key, and said, "Let's go." She pushed me off my seat and walked ahead to the elevator.

The man's room was on the second floor and smelled of aftershave and the cheap soap Rebecca loved. His suitcase took up the left side of the king-size bed, and pajamas lay bunched-up on the right.

"What if he comes back? Maybe he forgot his wallet?"

"You wanted this, didn't you?"

"Yes, sure, but…"

Becca shook her head. "Someone complained about loud noises coming from upstairs. I'm checking it out. I took you for protection."

Next to the bathroom sink lay a half-empty tube of Colgate and a ratty-looking toothbrush. The aftershave I smelled turned out to be called Musk. It wasn't so bad, I thought, but Becca made a disgusted face when I picked up the bottle.

There was nothing else to see in the bathroom, and the room itself had not been used much. So we carefully dug through the suitcase. "All his socks are black and all his underwear are white," I commented. Becca lifted up shirts and pants until she came up with a flask. She unscrewed the top and sniffed. "Whiskey," she said and took a swig. Then she started to undress.

I didn't ask what she was doing, I knew better than that. She stripped completely before grabbing the man's pajamas. They were too large, but she walked about the room looking pleased. "They're soft," she said. "Try." I grabbed one sleeve and felt the fabric. It was shiny polyester, drab green, but worn and washed so often it had lost some of its luster. Becca pulled me close and led me to the right side of the bed. I kept looking at the alarm clock on the nightstand, running calculations on how long dinner at Anthony's would take, how much time the man needed to find his way back to the motel. Rebecca kept her eyes closed. I noticed I was doing all the moving.

"He'll smell me," she said later, once we had settled again behind the reception desk. "But he won't know what happened. He won't be able to explain what he smells."

Something I wanted to ask since we had entered the man's room found its way back into my head. "Do you remember the winter four years ago? When the whole town was snowed in and the phone lines were dead? Some people lost their power and some old couple in the trailer park died?"

"Yeah." She drew the word out, turning it into a question.

"Do you remember a guy in an old white Grand Prix with racer stripes?"

She shrugged. "I don't look at people's cars. I don't care."

"That one was really loud. Massaged exhaust."

She shook her head. "Men."

"He wasn't very tall and wore a leather coat, and his hair was dark and curly. He said he'd been friends with my aunt when she was still around. Before she ran off with that construction worker. The guy's name was Paul. Katia kind of liked him, I think." I could see thoughts and memories shifting in Rebecca's head until she found a promising one and pulled it out to have a closer look.

"Did he wear cowboy boots?"

I nodded. "That's him. Do you know how long he stayed?"

She looked into the ceiling light and squinted. "He came after Christmas. I don't think he stayed longer than a night or two. Three max. He asked about my wedding book."

"Your wedding book?"

"Never mind. I threw it away the year after that. But he asked me about it and didn't laugh at me when I showed him. Only three or four other guests stayed here at the time. Christmas guests who couldn't leave because of the snow. Why?"

"He was at our house, asked for Opa. I just remembered him." I was reluctant to tell her about the car and how I had found it. "He never showed up again, even though we invited him for dinner."

"Your parents were already gone?"

I nodded.

"How old were you? Thirteen? Fourteen? And Katia was what? Sixteen or seventeen? And you wonder why he didn't want to have dinner with you?" She was laughing now, and indeed, from her perspective the whole encounter didn't make any sense.

"I guess," I said and dropped the topic. I wanted to cling to the memory of making love to Rebecca as long as I could, and her laughter was already chopping off small pieces of how it had felt to be with her. I could smell Musk on me and on her. For some reason I didn't think I could stand to face that hotel guest again.

Rebecca pulled a pair of rolled-up black socks from her pocket, took a pair of scissors from her desk drawer and cut a hole into one of them. I hadn't seen her steal them, wondered what she felt mutilating them. She said, "That winter you're talking about, your grandpa stayed with us for two nights as well. Said he drove off the road into a snowdrift."

"Opa stayed with you?"

"Yes, and I think he had a hooker with him. I didn't see her, but she was definitely with him. I heard them argue."

"We have hookers here? In this town?"

"Semi-pro," she answered. "How long has your grandma been dead?" She cut a hole into the second sock as well, then rolled them up again and put them next to the man's room key. She'd visit again, I knew, without me.

A few minutes later I left. I picked up some ice-cream at Fancy's and ate the whole quart after I got home. It came from a regional creamery and was called Zero Visibility to commemorate the blizzard from four years ago. What Rebecca had told me made me wonder how often Opa bought sex. "I needed a partner," he'd said, and maybe he was paying someone to play that role a few times a month. Perhaps his painting trips were just a cover for visits to bars and brothels. For the life of me I couldn't decide whether I hated or admired him for that. I wondered if he would let me have the Pontiac.

•

Katia's boyfriend Scott Hurme was working on a freighter over the holidays, and my sister agreed to celebrate Christmas with me and Mom. We hadn't bought a tree; all the exotic ones she'd planted in the fall lay dead and buried under icy snow. Maybe she didn't have the heart to kill another one.

On the twenty-fourth, she told us to pack a small bag and get in her car. Half an hour later we were on our way south. The heat in the Vega only came on reluctantly and dissipated quickly, and we all wore hats and coats and scarves. Whenever Katia or I asked about where we were going, Mom shook her head. She didn't seem happy. The corners of her mouth turned down in sharp creases, like those of a marionette.

By the time we stopped in St. Ignace I'd been asleep for a while. "Get out," Mom said. We abandoned the car, water stretched out in front of us, and I stumbled after Mom and Katia toward a small ferry boat.

"Where are we going?" I was annoyed, I was cranky. I wanted Julie, I wanted Rebecca, I wanted a soda. "What are we doing? Why are we getting on a boat?"

"This is your Christmas gift. This is all you're going to get," Mom said. "So enjoy it."

"Did I ask for this?"

Katia shot me a nasty look from over her shoulder. "Shut up."

My left leg had fallen asleep in the car, my hands were freezing. Fortunately, the small cabin on the ferry was heated, and I peeled off my coat and rubbed my face and ears. My body remained numb. "Mackinac Island?" I said.

The trip was short, no more than half an hour, and only about a dozen passengers climbed off the boat once we got there. Those were met by people in horse-drawn carriages or tricycles to carry luggage. We were met by no-one. Mom said, "I think it's this way," and headed out into the dark.

The Grand Hotel had closed in November, she told us, her words visible for a second or two in the cold before dissolving. A friend who ran a small bed-and-breakfast had invited her to stay. I was as bewildered by the news that Mom had friends as I was by trudging along a snowy path past the sleeping monster that was the Grand Hotel. We lowered our voices, we looked away and quickened our steps.

The house we approached a few minutes later had a warmly-lit porch, a Christmas tree out front and another one behind a large window on the first floor. And while Mom and Katia didn't break their stride until they had reached the wooden steps, I stayed behind and listened. There was not another sound in this world, I thought, and the two trees manifested the first real Christmas I had ever known. The one I had suspected other, better children were offered by better, kinder families. People who ate gingerbread cookies and were served hot chocolate in places where nobody had any cavities, and no one wore sweaty socks. I didn't wish to proceed, I didn't need to take a closer look. After the first moments of pure joy, disappointment already started to creep into my eyes. My presence in this house would make Christmas ordinary and insufferable.

A woman the same age as Mom came to the door and hugged our mother. What a strange spectacle that was. The woman laughed, said how long she hadn't seen her friend, hugged Katia, whom she had never met, and at last called out to me to come closer. "I'm Helen," she introduced herself, "and I've known your mom since we were together in elementary school and we both had a crush on the boy who was repeating third grade."

Inside, so many lights shone that it seemed I had been blindfolded for hours. Smells from the kitchen and what appeared to be the parlor hung about, layering, thickening the air. People I took to be other guests sat by the fireplace with wineglasses in their hands. They waved at us as though they'd been waiting for our arrival all day. My eyes teared up—I blamed the cold.

We dropped our bags in two rooms I barely looked at, then found ourselves at the kitchen table with Mom's friend Helen. She served mulled wine and told us her story of leaving her hometown and arriving on Mackinac Island with a man she barely knew, and how the love to that man hadn't lasted, but her love for the island had only grown.

Soon she was gone to talk to other guests and bring in more firewood, and Katia, Mom, and I looked at each other. I had only to glance at Mom's mouth of bark to feel the cold creep in. "So let's get this out of the way," she said. "I'm going to tell you my plan and you can ask questions, and then we'll shut up about it and enjoy Christmas."

•

The plan was not unlike trimming a bush with too many dead branches. You cut back, cut back some more, and hope that the bush will come out stronger, grow thicker, and turn leafy next spring. All she owned and what held her back was the house we lived in. Dad had signed the divorce papers, and she was now free to restart her life, sell the house, and return to Asia to work as a schoolteacher. She'd never wanted to leave Indonesia, and it was time to return to the one place on earth where she felt she belonged. Katia and I were the dead branches and would be cut.

Mom said that my sister needed to stand on her own two feet. Should she choose to go to college, she would receive a small stipend; Mom would entrust Opa Frank with some of the money the house sale would provide her with. It wouldn't be much, since she still owed him money he'd lent her to buy the house in the first place. As for me, Opa had agreed to take me in until graduation in June. I could choose to earn a scholarship and leave town or stay and work for a living. If I chose the former, I'd receive a bit of money from Mom.

"That's the plan," she concluded and got up to refill our glasses with mulled wine. "Why don't you guys stay here or go up to our rooms? I'd like to speak to Helen for a moment."

"Wait," Katia protested. "You said we could ask questions. We're not allowed to weigh in?"

"On my life? No."

"It's our life too. Why did you even come back if you just wanted to leave again? You should have stayed away. We were getting along just fine without you." Katia's cheeks grew redder still, painted with heat, wine, and fury. "You come back, screw everything up, and then abandon us a second time."

"Yes," Mom said. "It's not pretty. If I'd had it my way, your father and I would never have left town in the first place. Ever. But once we were on our way, it was actually me who didn't wish to return. Life is messy. I had you guys at a very young age; I wasn't ready for you and for living in that small town again. Your father hated every moment of it. That's why he became Mormon, that's why he insisted we leave. But that wasn't what he wanted either. Your father still hasn't found what makes him happy. I have, and I won't let go of it again. I'm not coming back a second time.

"You are right. You guys did well without us. So why can't you do it again? You have everything you need. If you want something, go after it. I won't be in your way." Her hand, when she picked up her glass, trembled. Her voice, though, was clear. No doubt clouded her eyes. "When I was seventeen, your Oma Anna took me to a psychic in Marquette. Maggie had left town already, and I think Oma wanted to know what path I might take and if she would lose her second daughter as well. She had no office, this psychic, but did readings in her home, in a bedroom that held a table, a floor lamp, three chairs, and nothing else. Her room wasn't what I had imagined. I wanted candles, crystal balls, I wanted her to wear a colorful kaftan and large earrings and dozens of bangles. Instead she wore a simple dress, no jewelry, no shoes. She asked my mother to leave after the first ten minutes in which she asked our names and ages and inquired about what I wanted to know. My mother was taken aback but said she would wait in the kitchen.

'Why do you want me to be alone with you?' I was afraid of this woman, even though she was barely taller than me, and not much heavier either.

'Because your mother will die soon and you will have to take care of your family and raise your brother, nurse your dad,' the woman said.

The room didn't seem so plain anymore. The walls started to move, as though they were made from paper and becoming unglued, shifting, undulating. I experienced vertigo. 'How?' I finally said.

'You'll get married.'

'Who is it?'

'You already know him, though he's with another girl right now. He's already in love with you. Your marriage won't be easy, but it is the right one for you. You will have four children. They won't look after you when you're old, they won't know you anymore. They'll refuse to see you.'

"This is what the woman in Marquette told me that day

while my mother waited in the kitchen. She waited until I didn't cry anymore, then led me to the bathroom to wash my face. Fancy glass vials with sour and bitter smelling liquids covered every surface. Incense was burning on the windowsill. I looked at my swollen face and red eyes, and my life seemed over. Why not kill myself, I thought on the way home, my mother smoking inside the car, only opening her window once in a while to let some of the smoke escape; it was too cold outside to do otherwise. Why not stop my life when I already knew how it would end?

"My mother didn't die. And I didn't marry until four years later when your dad, who I hadn't known until moving to Ann Arbor, got me pregnant. After both of you were born, we were done. He never laid hands on me again.

"Maybe the woman in Marquette had a good laugh after Mom and I cleared out. Maybe she put on a kettle and had a mug of hot tea. And yet I couldn't help but think that she knew my future as though it were the past and that she told me these inconceivable lies to push me onto a different path. She wanted to open my eyes to this life, and this was her way. I often wonder if she's still alive and if she remembers. I wonder if she would feel justified could she see me now, your dad gone, my children grown, leaving town once again."

I waited until Mom's face had relaxed once more. "Can't Katia and I stay in our house?" I asked. "At least until summer?"

Mom shook her head. "Opa has already found a buyer. We have until January 15." With that, she walked off to join her friend Helen.

•

Katia and I did not immediately leave the kitchen. We stared at our full glasses and looked for words that might fit the occasion, something that could make us feel better or at least describe how exactly we felt. But no matter how hard we tried we couldn't form any words that matched our thoughts. "All well, there is no hell," she finally said. "Let's go upstairs."

Mom and Katia had the bigger of the two rooms, but Katia, after getting her pajamas and toiletries, knocked on my door and climbed into bed with me. We killed the overhead light, stuffed pillows in our backs and sat in the near dark. Only the shine of the Christmas tree in the yard brightened the room.

"What are you going to do?" It was a stupid question and the only thing I could think of saying.

Katia leaned her head on my shoulder. "You know there is no family. It's an interesting find. It's all ours." She moved this way and that, repositioning her head. "You're so bony. I'm going to hurt myself." After that, her voice thinned to a whisper. "I don't think he'll ask me to marry him."

"Scott?"

"Who else?" Her nose nudged my neck. "Maybe I'll apply to State."

"Doing what?"

"I could be a nurse."

"You'd be good at that," I said.

"You think?"

"I don't know."

"Asshole," she breathed. "What are you going to do living with Opa in that cold house?"

"Maybe I can stay with Julie."

"Poor Julie."

"Who's the asshole now?"

"I've tested the goods—they're no good. And then, what will you do after graduation?"

I thought about what I had told Opa in that restaurant and repeated my words to Katia. "I can't feel anything," I said. "It's like being here with Mom, in this place. It doesn't make sense. It's pretty and shiny but it doesn't have anything to do with me. This place doesn't need me. It doesn't pay any attention to me and won't remember me."

"You're screwed up," she murmured.

"Are you in love with Rebecca?" Just then, we heard someone

walking up the stairs, a door opening, closing, and steps walking into the room next door. It had to be Mom, and we kept quiet and waited for a knock on our door. But after several minutes, everything fell silent. She must have gone to bed.

"She doesn't care," I said.

"I think I am." Katia's hands stopped moving.

I tried to figure out what I was feeling in response to her admission and couldn't. "Has she ever shown you the motel?" I said.

"What do you mean?"

"Has she ever taken you to one of the empty rooms?"

"Several times, yes."

I grabbed one of Katia's hands and imagined where it had been and what it had found. People touched and prodded and bumped and caressed one another, and they left so little behind. Then someone else would bump and caress them and get to hear the same moans, feel the same rough skin, the smell of armpits and bellies and feet. "She wants to leave," I said at last.

"I know."

"Has she asked you to come?"

Katia's breath ran over my skin without making a sound. I pulled my shoulder out from under her, pressed her onto the mattress and lay down on top of her, my head on her chest.

"Am I too heavy?" I asked.

"Too bony," she whispered. Then, "You're fine."

We stayed in that position until I couldn't tell anymore where we touched and where not. I fell asleep.

•

Mom didn't show at breakfast. Katia and I ordered eggs and toast from the menu. Her foot lay in my lap, and I ate one-handed, drank more coffee than I ever had. Two families unpacked gifts in the living area, and we heard them oohing whenever the tearing and crunching of paper stopped for a second.

"You want yours here or upstairs?" Katia wore my red sweater, the one that read 'Miners' on the front. It was too small for me and too small for her.

"You?"

"Here."

She pulled a small, wrapped something from her pajama pocket and put it next to my plate. I put my present onto hers. We sat and probed with our eyes. "Open it, potato face," she said at last.

It was a toy car, a purple metallic GTO. "Open yours," I said.

Hers was the exact same car, but green with yellow stripes. "Are you going to get me out of our town with that?" she asked.

I hadn't told her what Julie and I had found in Opa's shed, but I wasn't surprised by her gift. She knew I wanted a car, and Paul's Grand Prix, even though we had only ever seen it for maybe a minute or two, was always with us. An odd reference point of a time when we had been close. Yes, we'd had class-mates and friends, but we had made all decisions together, had spent most evenings by ourselves reading or listening to our parents' albums, and then, a bit later, our own.

"Thank you," we said at the same time and stuffed the cars back in our pockets. We waited an hour, then retrieved our coats from my room. "Do you have any money?" Katia asked.

I opened my wallet, another Christmas gift of hers, from three years back. I had two twenties that Opa had given me the weekend before. "Good," she said, and moments later we left the house. It was around ten, and the skies were waiting quiet and pale, naked, young, immensely marvelous, stretching out from above our heads onto the water. It wasn't as cold as it had been the night before; the old snow was slippery and our steps small and quick, our arms spread wide. Christmas trees were still glowing and looked cheap and disheveled. The Grand Hotel squinted in the light. Before long, we were at the water's edge and stomping through brown, frozen grass.

"Where are we going?" I said.

"To the ferry."

"What for?"

She shook her head and wouldn't talk while we were waiting for the boat to arrive. Once we were back in St. Ignace, we found Mom's Vega, and Katia pulled the keys from her coat pocket, and the engine started on the second try.

4

"It might not run properly anymore. Was in rough shape then and will be in worse shape now."

"Why did you buy the Pontiac if you weren't going to drive it?" My skin smelled of Julie, and as long as I could find her scent on my clothes, questioning my grandfather felt like a mountain I could scale. As long as I could smell her, I knew I needed a car.

The new year remained brittle, and only Mom welcomed the cold and snow and each new gray morning. Each new day she spent carrying things to the curb and packing several old leather bags with clothes and strange knickknacks she'd brought home from her mission. One morning, the kitchen sink was full of broken glass. When I lifted out a delicate stem, I recognized that these were the wine glasses my dad had loved. Mom had complained that her hands wouldn't fit through the narrow opening and that she feared breaking them while doing the dishes and slicing her hand open. I left them where they were, I hadn't even heard a single sound. All her preparations Mom conducted in silence. She offered me so much of it in those days that I gave in to every hint or wink just to hear her speak again. Or I simply left the house. I left a lot that winter.

Julie said that her parents had a tenant renting the small apartment above their garage. By spring, he would be gone. "Do you want it? I told them you needed a place to stay, and since we're in school together, they'd be okay if you paid a little less." I told her I would think about it.

Opa Frank's right foot was in a cast after he'd broken a bone by tripping over a tree root. It was a source of deep shame for him that he'd been forced to seek help from Dr. Television in the matter. Not only that, but he had to cut back on his schedule and sent his patients Koren's way. Snow once again covered streets and sidewalks in our town, and Opa mostly stayed indoors. He couldn't drive, walking caused him pain. His mood had darkened over the holidays but at least he was willing to talk.

"Why did you buy the car?" I asked again.

Opa said, "He needed money, and I took pity on him."

"So he was the construction worker Maggie ran off with?"

He nodded.

This was news to me, but in hindsight it appeared odd that Katia and I hadn't asked Paul about his relationship with Maggie. "Why didn't he tell us? He only said they'd been close. At first we thought he was Mom's old boyfriend." I thought about the situation, which was difficult when Opa Frank kept his eyes on me. Thick glasses enlarged them grotesquely. "But you hated him for stealing Maggie," I said before I could use more diplomatic language. I looked away from his face and into the beef stew Mom had made so I could carry it over to the old man. I had warmed it up for the two of us and hadn't forgotten to bring bread and crackers. Opa provided the beer.

He stopped eating and sighed. But it took him another minute or two before he said, "People make mistakes in their lives."

"So you regret that you disowned her?"

He looked at me as though I were a crystal ball revealing my every thought to him. I felt that he could have taken my heart, my lungs, or my ribs just by reaching across the table—the way he reached for bread and salt—and neither my skin nor my own will could have prevented him from grabbing what he wanted.

"I don't know what got into me back then. I was younger, though not young, and she was my firstborn. I wanted her to be all the things she could achieve and—I admit it—the ones I thought she should achieve. If you'll ever have children, you might feel similarly when they slowly slip your grasp. Right now, you are slipping from your Mom's grasp. Parents guide their children for so many years and dream so many dreams for them, but they know nothing about the dreams their children have. I didn't know anything. Maybe Anna suspected things, but not me."

"Mom doesn't have any dreams for me," I said.

Opa nodded. "Maybe not. Maybe…" Then he said, "I overreacted. Paul—you met him—he wasn't a bad guy. He just wasn't the right man for Maggie. That's what I thought—what I thought I knew—at the time. I can be a mean bastard. I know that, always have. But I hated that man and his profession and his small dreams. That car said everything I needed to know about him.

"But he did love my daughter, and she loved him. I should have helped them, I really should have. Yet I was hurt. I didn't want to lose that beautiful daughter of mine to a man who could never achieve what she could have achieved so easily. I didn't want her to be tied to somebody who couldn't hold down a steady job and who moved from state to state in a garish car and cowboy boots.

"But I was wrong. I was wrong. I had it all wrong. She didn't tie herself to him. I did. If I had welcomed him into this house and into this family, once things soured, she would have returned home."

He looked very old in that moment. The light, which was fading already, threw a web of shadows over his face, black spreading along the creases of his skin. He wasn't a bad-looking man, but in the moment he picked up his spoon once more to dip it into the stew and abandon it there, he stopped being Opa Frank and turned into an old man I pitied for his jowls and loose neck.

"She left him somewhere in Arizona. A year or two after he took her away from me. They had a fight, and she left their apartment with nothing but her clothes, wallet, and keys. He thought she'd be back by dark, but she never returned home.

He received a postcard from California a few days later. It bore a picture of the La Brea tar pits. No address, no nothing."

"Did he go and look for her?"

"He did. At least that's what he says. But he couldn't locate her. Two years later he got married for the first time. They stayed together for about ten years, moved across the country and got divorced in Oklahoma. He married a second time, but that relationship ended quickly."

The old man fell silent, and I got up as quietly as I could, as though he were asleep and I couldn't risk waking him.

"Get me some too," he said when I returned with more stew. "And get us more beer."

Once he'd opened his bottle, he continued. "He never forgot her. In a way, I guess, we suffered similar fates. We got angry and possessive, and Maggie decided she didn't want any of it. Paul and I are very different people, but we both found out that we couldn't own Maggie. She knew what she wanted and couldn't be held back.

"In any case, even after two marriages, Paul never forgot about Maggie, and four years ago he decided he needed to find her. Since he hadn't heard from her in almost twenty years, he got it into his head that he had to make the drive. For whatever reason, he thought she might have returned home. He didn't want to spend another Christmas without her, he said."

"Why didn't he just call you?" But as soon as I had asked, I remembered what Paul had said the night he came to our house. "He said he called you many times."

Opa Frank nodded. "I don't know if he had the right number. Or if he called when I was at the office. I don't know why he didn't call at work. I could have saved him the trip. But I think that maybe he just is the kind of guy who needs to see for himself. He's a romantic for sure. He said he didn't sell the car because it was the one he owned when he fell in love with Maggie. If he hadn't been broke, he wouldn't have parted with it. And he sure is proud. I offered to loan him the money, but he insisted I take the car. I was her father—though God knows I didn't act like one—so at least, in some sense, he said, it would stay in the family."

"Did you guys meet at the motel? You must have stayed there around the same time."

"Why would I stay at that place?" He looked at me with open contempt before his features softened again. "Yes, you're right. My accident. It took a while to get the car towed. No, no, I didn't see him there, though I guess we could have run into each other."

"You didn't just walk home?" I couldn't bring myself to mention the prostitute.

He paused for just a second. "My secret is out, isn't it? That Karvonen girl gave it away?"

"I'm sorry," I said. "She just mentioned it."

"Another thing I'm not proud of. Yes, I was with company, disreputable company. It was an awful, awful situation, and she made a scene too. I was weak, there really is no excuse. Anna would turn in her grave if she knew."

The mention of his wife hung about like thick smoke and choked Opa. I held my breath, waited for it to clear. "Where is he now?" I asked. "Paul?"

"California, I guess. That's where he was headed, he said."

"On the Greyhound?"

"I didn't want the car. He said I must take it. What would I do with that old beast?"

"How much did you give him?"

"Too much."

"If I earned enough, would you let me buy it from you?"

Opa Frank looked at me for a long time. He wiped his mouth meticulously, checking the napkin for traces of stew. He smiled, and maybe it was a sad smile, but it grew harder to tell since the shadows now obliterated his face; we still hadn't switched on the lights in the dining room. "But you want to drive it right away, I guess?"

I nodded. "I'll pay for any repairs it might need."

"There's no need. I can have it fixed up at the shop."

I sat in the gray light of Opa's house but was miles away, my ears full of noise, the windows rolled down, Rebecca next to me with her long feet on the dashboard. I didn't thank my grandfather until minutes later, when I got up to clear away the dishes.

"Only one condition," he said. "I feel rather bad about this business. It's not that...it's not that it's a secret. Everybody in this town knows that Maggie ran off. But people don't need to know the car belonged to Paul. I bought it for you is all."

I nodded. If he'd demanded I swear a solemn oath I would have done that too.

He took off his glasses and set them down on the table. "Well, and there's one more condition. If Maggie returns one day, the car will be hers. No ifs and buts."

•

Our house closed on January 15, and on the same day, through freezing rain, I drove Mom to the Marquette airport. Her Vega had more rust than metal by then and it was on its third engine. She told me to keep it after she'd taken her three bags from the trunk and backseat. Before she stepped from the small waiting area onto the tarmac, where drenched passengers were already climbing stairs to board the plane, she shook my hand and said, "It's been interesting to get to know you. I don't expect to meet you again, so take care of yourself. Have a nice-enough time on this planet. You might fit in. You're not a horrible person."

Then she turned and walked through the swinging glass doors, and I stared after her. She didn't stop to wave, didn't look over her shoulder. Outside in the short-term parking lot the car wouldn't start, and I called Katia, who wasn't home, and then Miles, who picked me up in a friend's truck two hours later. "How did it go?" Miles asked. "I don't know what I would do if Mom left me."

"She just came back to fuck everything up for me," I said. "If not for her misfortune, I'd be a heavenly person today." It started to rain even harder then, and the road ceased to exist in front of our eyes. It took us an hour to tow the Vega to a junkyard, where I sold it for twenty-five dollars.

•

Because it had the bath next door, I was given Opa Frank's office for a bedroom. He told me he'd considered moving downstairs because of his age but decided he needed the exercise of climbing stairs more than me.

I was almost nineteen and had grown up on this very street. I was only moving a few yards to the left, and still, after school, when Miles and I transferred the contents of my room to Opa Frank's old office, they looked all wrong. They carried dust I had never noticed before. Sweaters and pants showed new holes. Things Katia had given me lost their meaning. Miles would hold up books and jackets, and I couldn't remember if they were mine. Opa's house was built from ammonia and soap, from white tiles and shower heads, from stainless steel and sulfur. Once you were inside, you couldn't hold on to who you were or wanted to be. In his house, I'd be forever the small boy in the back of the red coupe, cold and full of snot, not belonging to anyone. This was merely a spot where my body could be stored with relative ease. The body needed to be taken care of, be protected from harm.

At the end of February, the mechanic Opa had hired told him it'd be only another few days until he would have my car ready. Around that same time, Katia picked me up one afternoon in her boyfriend's Monte Carlo and she paid for spaghetti at Anthony's. She looked all pretty, extra scrubbed. She'd gotten new contacts, she said. Her acne scars were safely tucked under a layer of make-up. I fidgeted and cast down my eyes; hers were so loud it hurt.

"You have a plan," I said. "You're going to tell me after we're done eating, and then I can ask questions but I won't be able to change a thing."

This made her laugh, and before we got our food she was

crying, and a contact slipped from her eyeball, and we searched the table and then the floor. The spaghetti was served, and the waitress helped us with our search and found the contact right next to the glass of ice water. Katia put in the contact again, but it wasn't right, maybe there was dust or grit on it or crumbs from whoever had eaten at that table before us—Anthony's wasn't the place where a sauce stain or a few crumbs made the waiters change the tablecloth. In any case, something was rubbing, and soon her eye turned red and between bites of spaghetti, she took out the contact once more, blew on it, dunked it into the ice water, and tried it again.

"So when are you leaving?" I asked. "You're not going to abandon me while I'm living with Opa?"

"How is that going? Is it weird?"

"It's weird that I can see our house from the kitchen window, and there are new people living there already, and when they see me, they barely say Hello and they don't even know that their little asshole children are now living in my room and that they're sleeping in the same big bedroom we slept in for years."

That last remark made Katia cry again, but she held her face up so she wouldn't lose her contacts again. "I'm sorry," she said. "Yes, that was our house. It belonged to us."

The waitress came and asked if everything was okay, because Katia was crying harder now, and in response to that question my sister choked on the spaghetti and started to cough and got up and ran to the bathroom.

There was little light left in the dining room, orange like old celluloid. I ate my plate of food and later Katia's food as well. When my sister returned from the bathroom, her make-up was mostly gone and her face looked splotchy. She looked at her empty plate without making a comment. "I'm scared," she said. "I'm scared I'll never see you again."

"You don't even like me that much," I said.

"True, but you're the only one who knows me. Leaving you is like burning all the photos anybody ever took of me and my family. I'll live in another city, and there'll be nothing left of my life here."

"Isn't that a good thing?" I said.

She nodded. "But I'm scared anyway. That there's not enough me in me. You know, not enough to make anyone recognize me. Ever."

A bit later she paid, and we left the restaurant. Katia started the Chevy, but we didn't go anywhere. She just put the heat on high and put her head in my lap. I stroked her hair, and she said, "Thank you," and then something else that I didn't catch. I wanted to know what she'd said, but I knew that I couldn't repeat the moment and that she would grow self-conscious if I asked.

We sat like this for over an hour. She put a hand under my sweater, and I put one under hers. "You'd be crazy not to go." I felt awful for saying that and was certain she wanted me to. "Should we go to your place?"

She shook her head. "He's home."

"Does he know?"

She shook her head again. "I'm awful."

"So when are you going to leave?"

"Tomorrow," she said. "I'm all packed. She's going to take her grandma's old car and pick me up."

"They fixed it up? What will Ingri say?"

"I don't know. She can't drive anymore."

"She loves that car."

"Well, that's how we're going to get out of here."

Pain made me twist in my seat. I opened the door, abandoned the head in my lap and started to walk. Two or three minutes later, the Chevy appeared at my side. "Get in, potato face," she said. It would have been the right choice, the fair choice to do that, but I needed to show her how much I was hurt. So I started to run and when I had the chance, cut through a back alley where she couldn't follow. I expected her to be waiting at Opa's house, and when I finally got there, twenty or thirty minutes later, the Chevy wasn't there. Instead, another car stood by the curb. At first I didn't understand, and it took me a while to see what had happened. Yes, it was Paul's Grand Prix, but it hadn't been merely checked, cleaned, and repaired. The white paint was gone, the racing stripes were gone. Instead it was a glossy black. I stood and gaped. And then I sat down on the snowy street and couldn't stop shivering until I got too cold to even shiver.

5

Opa turned seventy in March. The cast on his foot had long been removed, and every morning he rose at six, had a breakfast of coffee and two slices of toast, and left the house by seven. Once or twice a month, he'd take an entire weekend off to drive to Saginaw or even Ann Arbor, "to be among people." On those weekends, Julie stayed with me. After making love, she'd sometimes go and play the piano in the living room. She only remembered a few songs from the time her parents had paid for lessons, and I sat on the couch and listened, slightly embarrassed by the noise of a long-mute instrument. Julie had such short, deaf fingers.

On the first fluke spring day, while the next snowstorm was waiting just around the corner, the warmth made my skin feel too small. In the streets of our town, men scratched their necks and bellies, women plotted their next move. And because my limbs tingled all over, and Julie had said she didn't have time for me after school, I took Opa for a drive. After he arrived home around six, it was still warm enough for me to forego a jacket and only wear a T-shirt that belonged to Katia and was a bit tight. This was a few days after his birthday, a Saturday, which he'd celebrated by driving south to Bay City.

"Where are we going?" he asked once he'd climbed into the car.

"Nowhere." I hoped it didn't sound stupid. "We can have dinner somewhere if you want, but I thought we could just drive for a while."

Opa rolled down the window and laughed, moving his hand as though he wanted to grip a piece of the wind. "This isn't so bad, is it?"

"Yeah," I said.

"Jack did all right? There's rust, he says, but the engine is in good shape."

I nodded. "Why did you paint it? What was wrong with the old paint?"

"You don't like the paint?"

I thought about it. "It looks too good for me."

For a moment, his right hand formed a fist. Then he spread the fingers, stretching them as though they were achy and stiff. "You like this girl you're running around with? Is it serious? She's the type who will look stumpy when she hits thirty. The thinner they are, the better they look later, believe me."

I didn't answer. We were in the center of town, passing Sparcky's. Opa pointed and said, "That's her right there, isn't it?"

Several people stood outside of Fancy's, dazed, as if they'd awoken from a deep sleep, blinking their eyes, rubbing their white arms and pasty faces. Julie was among them, clinging to a tall guy with coiffed hair and a face grandmothers could trust. He bent down to kiss her, and she closed her eyes and put a hand on his cheek.

"That's her," I said. "And that's her boyfriend. He sells weed. Mark X, they call him."

"I've treated him since he was a toddler. Mark Sellers. His parents are both short. I still don't know how they produced this giant."

Of course I knew Julie spent time with her boyfriend. She'd never lied about that. I'd seen them together before, but my grandfather hadn't been sitting in the seat next to me. Thankfully, Opa Frank didn't say another word about them. Instead he asked, "How do you feel about raising a family?"

"With Julie?"

"Well, that might not be up to you. No. How do you feel about finding the right one and raising a family? Taking on responsibility, taking a job, having kids?"

"I'm in high school," I said.

"Not for much longer. Will you accept a scholarship?"

I'd been offered to play Division III football. One school was only a few hours south, the other was in Ohio. They were partial scholarships; I hadn't convinced anyone to give me a free ride. "I've been thinking about it."

"Let's drive north, toward the water. If that's okay," he added quickly.

At the end of Main Street, I turned onto the county road and stepped on the gas. The engine roared and crackled.

"I'm getting old," Opa said. "Mind you, I could live to a hundred. But I could also die any day of some organ failure or other."

I opened my mouth to say something stupid, but he waved me off. "I could die tonight in this car. With your mom and sister gone, I have only you to rely on."

"I don't understand," I said.

"Yes, yes, you do. We're the last of the Holmstroms, even though that's not your last name. If you leave town this summer, I'm a seventy-year-old doctor near retirement in a house that's too big for him and no family to give him some beef stew if he breaks a leg."

I thought about that. I didn't pity him. I don't think I was even a bit concerned. He had money, he could pay anyone in town to cook and clean for him. "Why did you never look for Maggie?"

Opa Frank sucked in his lips until there was only a small slit left where his mouth had been. Then he said, "I did. I scoured phone books and newspapers. I even hired a private detective once—your grandmother suggested it and would have given me hell if I hadn't. She left no trace. Maybe she took a different name. Maybe she left the country. There are so many ways to make yourself disappear."

I thought about ways to make oneself disappear. I had heard from Katia only once since she'd left town. Scribbled on a postcard of the World Trade Center were the bare facts. She lived with Becca in Manhattan. They'd moved from Rebecca's friend's loft into an apartment in Chelsea and she worked as a waitress and went to auditions and open mics.

"She might have children," Opa said. I must have looked funny at him, because he repeated the sentence. "If she found someone she truly loved and had children with him, I might have more grandchildren than just you and your sister. It's haunting me that I'm living uselessly when I could be with her children, help raise them. It's awful."

I nodded. Maggie became Katia, and I watched her disappear among cartoonish high-rises. Paul had appeared and disappeared again, Opa hadn't been able to hold on to Maggie, I hadn't been able to keep any family near me. "There was a woman, the day before Paul arrived." I tried to describe her to Opa. What if Maggie had tried to come home? Then Paul would have missed her by less than twenty-four hours that winter. It was heartbreaking and romantic to think he'd come so close to finding her. It was the kind of story I wished for Julie and me, though we had too much of each other and too little; our love didn't seem destined for snowstorms and deep regrets.

Opa Frank listened, asked about details, then finally shook his head. "I haven't seen her in twenty years, but I don't know, it doesn't sound like her. And why wouldn't she have asked about me and Grandma? It doesn't feel right." I admitted it didn't sound right, but I wasn't ready to let go of my story yet. Then I remembered the shoes she'd worn. "She wore pumps," I said out loud. "As though she was attending a party."

"She must have lived in the neighborhood. A visitor maybe. Everybody was stranded."

A daughter returning to her home in the middle of a blizzard—the story was too farfetched and dramatic for our town. "You could move south," I said at last.

"Where to?"

"You'd be among people."

With his left, he punched my shoulder. "Don't get smart with me," he said. "We're flesh and blood, as much as we don't want to believe that. We need company. But truly, I'm worried about my last years on this planet. Nobody down south gives a rat's ass about me. Yes, it's nice to see strange faces once in a while, but when you're close to the end of your life, you want some familiar faces near you. You and I, we won't stare at each other and confess our undying love. We're cut from the same cloth. We observe and keep to ourselves. Sure you hang around that girl. You're young, after all. That's just nature demanding her due. But I don't see anybody else come and visit you.

"We're not so very different. But you can't piss your life away taking care of your grandpa, I get that." I was expecting his speech to continue, but he stopped talking. There wasn't much traffic on the road. Heading north, I tried to conjure Julie, but my mind went numb whenever I replayed Mark kissing her. No car was loud enough to make me feel a thing.

At last he spoke again, raising his sharp voice over the din of the engine. "I'll give you a week to decide on my offer."

"What offer?"

"I'll buy the next year from you. I'll pay you a decent wage. You don't have to do much for it, but you keep living in my house. You help with repairs—the house is at the end of its maintenance cycle—but otherwise you can do what you want. You don't have to sit with me in the evenings and hold my hand. You can be yourself. You can sleep in and date that girl, whatever. But you give me one year."

"I might be in town anyway," I said.

"I know your girlfriend's family offered to rent you a room above their garage. Your mom had a hunch you might stay with them. I don't want that."

I couldn't make sense of what he said, and the evening sucked the warmth out of the car with sudden greed. I rolled up my window, turned on the heat, and after ten minutes the lake appeared in front of us. Enough light was left to show how vast the expanse of water was. The waves were choppy, the wind gusty—I could feel it grabbing the car. "One year?" I said, just to say something.

"And you have until next week to decide."

"One week."

Opa nodded. "I have cancer. Chronic lymphocytic leukemia. Leukemia for geezers. It won't kill me just yet, it's slow, but I need to prepare for the future. Treatment, maybe a nursing home further down the road. I need to plan, and your presence would help." He paused, took off his glasses, and wiped them with his shirt. "That's an awful lot of water. You could drown our whole town in it."

•

"He's here," she whispered. I had just returned from a chips-and-beer run in the Grand Prix and found Julie sitting at one end of my bed with the covers tightly draped around her. "He's come back." My desk lamp provided the only light; it'd been dark for hours. Temperatures had dropped again, but there was no snow in the forecast.

"His car isn't outside." I was whispering too, immediately feeling ridiculous. "And so what? It's not like he's some monster."

"I saw him walking down the hallway. I had just come out of the bathroom. I don't think he heard me or saw me."

"And?"

"Where is he now? He's not making a sound."

"He's in Ann Arbor. He left yesterday."

"Maybe he came back early."

"But where is his car?"

"How would I know?" Her face regained its color. When I'd left, she'd been flushed, her neck damp, her clothes tangled in the sheets. "Is he trying to stalk us? Is he getting off on hiding in his house and listening in on us?"

I put chips and beer on my desk, on an argumentative paper

about homicide and the death penalty. "I'll check it out." Whatever her concerns were, they weren't mine. Still, I understood that closing and locking the door wouldn't work. Her face said so. I wasn't certain what she felt, but I could read the level of those feelings. Of course I left the room.

In bare feet I walked down the narrow hallway to the front of the house. "Opa?" I shouted. Katia and I had never found him that winter day four years prior, instead inventing stories of his tragic demise. How much less interested I was now in finding him. No adventure, just the perfunctory attempt to locate Opa so my girlfriend would sling her arms around me again and stay the rest of the night.

"Opa." I gave the word an extra syllable, my shout charging up the stairs and coloring the air. I'd turned the heat to seventy-two degrees earlier that evening, but it felt colder now, and when I checked the thermostat, the small red arrow had returned to sixty-five. Maybe he had been here? But why?

I checked his upstairs bedroom. No suitcase, no wrinkles in his sheets. No Opa Frank. It didn't smell of his aftershave.

"He's definitely not here," I said when I returned to my room. I didn't touch Julie yet. It would take some minutes for her to trust me again, to trust the house and the quiet. I put a new album on the turntable, one my sister had given me. Neil Young, who I only tolerated because he conjured Katia, made me smell her, made me turn my head because I thought I'd seen her sitting on my desk chair or standing by the closet.

"You like that stuff?" Julie said.

"Sure. Sometimes."

She nodded. "You don't believe me, right?"

"I do," I said, and was surprised to find it was true. "But he's not here."

"How can you believe what I'm saying and at the same time think he's not here?" She wasn't angry, she wanted to know.

I shook my head. "It doesn't make sense, I guess."

"No. No, it doesn't."

"Do you believe in the afterlife?" I sat down on the desk chair, grabbing a beer, wheeling closer to her but staying off the bed. It would be minutes before I could attempt to touch her.

"Heaven, you mean?"

"Any kind, really."

"I hope so. I mean, I don't know. I don't think there's milk and honey, but yeah, maybe there's a white light and peace forever."

"Mom told me about Zen Buddhism once. After she came back and before she was planting her trees. In Zen, there is no afterlife, just a void. That's what I believe. It's black and empty and there's no thought, you don't even know you're dead. It's like you have never even been here." I remembered to make a pause before my next thought. "But I also believe that I'll be reborn as a dog. Then maybe a plant after that. That we go through all kinds of iterations until we've had enough."

She waited for more, but I was done. Her mouth stood open. "That's nonsense. You can't believe one and the other at the same time."

"But I do. I really do. I can't explain it, but it makes sense. And that's how I know that you saw Opa and also that's he's not here. I just know."

Julie got up on her knees and held her hands out. Then, after I'd sat down next to her, she took hold of the sides of my face and shook me and laughed and planted kisses on my face. "You idiot. You silly, silly, idiot."

I didn't play her, I swear I didn't play her, and yet, every step of the way I knew what to say and how to say it, and when she finally let go of the sheet and revealed that she'd never gotten dressed, I knew what was next and next after that. It wasn't feeling. Cunning maybe; I had figured her out.

•

Little of what I feel I can properly name. I'm bad with definitions and tags and affixing them to what goes through my head or what gives me a stomach ache or what makes my cheeks blush in company and turn my eyes toward the tips of my feet. There's a vocabulary for this, but words and what goes through my head and paralyzes me or makes me break out in a sweat don't easily join. When people say 'love' or 'rage' or 'sadness,' I of course understand what they mean, and yet, they treat them as absolutes, as though these emotions had the weight and easy shape of bricks and could be spotted and used for building arguments.

I register everything that happens within me, but it's like walking through a park with trees and bushes and flowers and everything is blooming, but you can't name a thing. And maybe you have a few names you learned and attach them randomly to what you see. You can't ever be sure you're right, but you still know that what you see is really there. Only that when you talk about that park to anyone else, nothing makes sense anymore.

But no, it's not like that all. How can you describe a blooming purple bush hit by a stray beam of light next to yellow flowers, and somebody has discarded a light-blue t-shirt on the ground and in the distance, you hear the bell of a passing bike? What word do you use for that? How do you explain what you're seeing to someone who wants you to say 'birch tree,' 'magnolia,' and 'beautiful'?

·

In early April I received a letter from Katia. Rebecca had left, she didn't know where to, and my sister had to give up their apartment and now lived in a single room with two other women, in a walk-up on the upper Westside. She asked how I was, she asked what I was going to do. There was no address on the envelope. I pinned the letter to my wall, as though it was her voice and body and smell I could pin up there and keep around. I loved the curves of her writing, the smeared ink. I imagined her walking through Central Park. I imagined her getting hit by a truck as she was crossing 59th Street, and I felt my body go numb. My sister was the last person to remember me. Without her, I would be gone.

I felt ashamed that I had thought Rebecca could be in love with me. In my imagination, she'd been the one that got away. In my imagination I had provided her with something only I knew how to give. Bathing her grandmother, slapping her face and thighs when she told me to, rummaging through the motel guest's belongings—I'd thought I was special and that the importance she'd had for me I also had for her. By now I understood that she probably couldn't remember my name anymore and had forgotten my face. I'd been a boy who had been available. Not even a cherished one.

One Friday after school, Julie got into my car and said that her parents' tenant, the one who had rented the small apartment above their garage, had finally moved out. "You still want it? They say they want to meet you first, but you don't have to pay a security deposit."

"I have a place to stay," I said.

She changed her face to a rigid one, not unlike Mom's when she wanted you to dig a bigger hole for her tree than was necessary. "That house is creepy." She'd only been over to my place a couple of times after the night she thought she'd seen Opa wandering the hallway. She'd refused to stay the night since then. Mark was suspicious, she said, we needed to cool it, she said, but I knew that wasn't the reason.

"When do I have to let them know?" I asked. "My Opa is pretty old, and I've told him I'd stay another year."

"Why?"

"Why what?"

"He's not that ancient. He's still working. It's not like he's going to die any minute. And you'd still be living in town."

I had promised Opa not to tell anyone about his condition, but Julie needed an explanation. "He's got cancer and wants me to help him get his things in order."

"I'm sorry," she said. "That's awful. But you can see him every day even if you stay with us."

I wasn't getting anywhere arguing with her. I looked at my

hands on the steering wheel, at the broad nails that needed trimming, and even though it didn't make any sense, I said, "When can I have a look at it?"

"Day after tomorrow," she said.

"Do they know about us?"

Julie shook her head, her hair flying about her face. Her eyes stayed open, sunburst dials, brown they were, I remember them now, light making them gleam for short moments. Then she kissed me quickly and got out of the car again. "Mark is picking me up in ten."

I watched her walk away, getting lost among other students, other legs and arms and heads getting in the way and eating her up. My ears were full of static. I put the car in gear and turned onto Main Street. The sun just barely made her way through the clouds. Nothing seemed to have a shadow, every building, every tree seemed flat, painted without much care or craft. It was the kind of weather for premonitions, as though your mind conjured it up, or as if the weather commented on the plans you had made and let you know that your life and dreams were just guesses and not very good ones at that.

If I stayed with Opa, I would have enough money to get by. I could think about the next steps in my life and buy myself time. If I moved to Julie's, I'd need a job. I'd work in a town where nobody had any plans. Nobody who stayed ever thought beyond Fancy's or the hardware store. Julie would get a job with St. Mary's School for the Deaf in the fall, where her father worked as vice-principal. St. Mary's was a thirty-minute drive away, in a somewhat larger town. They had a movie theater and several grocery stores and a few bars. She'd been looking for apartments, but her parents wanted her to stay until she got settled into her job.

I drove past Opa's house, barely looking at the empty driveway, the gray siding, the deep porch. I didn't feel like getting out of the car just yet. Instead, I decided to take a detour through the outskirts of our town. The light was even less merciful on the dirt roads, pointing at dilapidated houses with junk cars, junk machinery, and just plain junk lining the property, large dogs running into the road to bark at the Grand Prix and follow it for a while. American flags were everywhere, tied to make-shift poles and large pick-ups with rusted-out bodies. What do you see? the sun seemed to ask. Am I not clear enough? Even staying another day past graduation is nonsense. You can't move in with that girl. She's not your girlfriend. Forget about her. She'll forget about you the minute you're gone.

By the time I finally returned to Opa's house, his car stood in the driveway, trunk open. I saw him vanish into the house with two large grocery bags, and there were more in his car. Hadn't we just stopped at the Supa-Save to get what we needed? Had he invited guests?

After I parked out front and locked the door, I noticed the other car pulling to the curb past our driveway. It wasn't our new neighbor—I knew the old Impala cruiser and who sat behind the wheel. As if to say 'I told you so,' the sun removed herself and left everything around me gray.

Mark was not alone. Two of his friends, Tony and Skip also got out, but they only stood by the open doors, watching Mark approach me. And I couldn't help it—even though I knew this was going to get ugly quick, I felt flattered. Mark, the weed dealer, Mark X, felt threatened enough to pay me a visit.

"Hey," I said.

"She told me everything, you little fuck."

He stopped a few feet away from me, not close enough to throw a punch. Still, I could feel the pain of three pairs of fists and feet already. I couldn't understand why Julie would have told him about us; she'd just asked me to move into her parents' apartment. Had my hesitation offended her? My voice sounded a bit squeaky, a bit shaky, but I said, "It's not that little. She probably didn't want to upset you."

Tony and Skip approached fast, but Mark was faster. I lifted my arms in defense, but his punch sailed right through them and hit me just below my ribs. Then his knee dug itself into my crotch. There was no air left in my entire body and I went down, balling up. The smell of exhaust grew overwhelming.

"What the hell?" I heard a voice call from somewhere beyond our small group. A shoe landed on my elbow, another stomped on my leg. Then Mark said, "What do you want, Grandpa?"

Tony and Skip laughed. A car door opened, followed by a clanging noise. Skip said, "Look at you. Whoa, now."

For the time being, the three had forgotten about me, and I turned my face enough to see Opa Frank with an aluminum bat approaching the sidewalk. Mark raised an arm as if to say, Wait a minute, but Opa Frank kept going. The bat struck Mark's knee, the second hit crashed into the side of his face. Then it was Skip's turn.

I gasped, and, holding on to the Grand Prix, got to my feet. Mark tried to do the same, but I kicked him in the mouth. I didn't stop even after he went down again, even after his nose was broken. Opa stood on the sidewalk, waiting for Tony's advance. Tony's hat lay in the street, wind blowing it toward the next driveway. He was holding his arm.

"Can you drive?" Opa asked him.

Tony nodded without making a sound.

"Tell you what. You load up your two friends here and get lost." He took a step toward Tony, who backed away before helping Skip with his good arm open the car door and scramble inside. It took him longer to get Mark back on his feet. Skip couldn't find the keys and had to rummage through Mark's pockets. I was thinking of Julie and what she would say if I ever saw her again.

Once the old cruiser had turned around and left, Opa threw the bat into his trunk and told me to help him with the groceries. "And why did those guys show up? Girl trouble?"

"Thank you," I said.

"You shouldn't hit a guy once he's down, but screw it, I'm sure Mark deserved it."

I wasn't sure he did, but it had felt good. Unhinged, wild, and good. As though for once I knew what to do and could do it. "What do we need those for?" I asked, grabbing a bag full of cans. Pasta, soup, meats.

"Just stocking up. I went overboard, didn't I?"

"Yeah, you did." I grinned even though my lip was numb and I tasted blood. "You totally did." I felt connected to something so strong, you could never ever break it. In that moment, I wanted to stay another year with him, money or not. I was so grateful, I felt ashamed. The chill of our winters will be in me to my dying day.

6

"Oh, you're back." Miles was growing a beard, but his chin showed considerable gaps and blank spots. "Heard about Mark. You're out of girlfriends at the moment, huh? Is that why you remember me?" He did hold open the door, though, and I entered without replying, followed him up the wooden stairs to his room, the door marked with stickers he'd collected since we were in kindergarten.

Sheet music, insects on tightly strung wires, lay on Miles's unmade bed, shirts and pants and socks on the carpet. "Want some water?" he asked.

I shook my head. "Just thought I'd stop by."

"I can see that." He sat down on the bed. "What's new?"

I shook my head, took some books off his desk chair. The second I sat down, I felt uncomfortable, as though Miles had left pushpins on the cushion and they were now digging into my flesh, as though the room were full of boxes and I could barely make out my friend from behind the cardboard. "Nothing, really. Opa has to appear in court."

Miles laughed. "Didn't you want to move into Julie's parents' apartment?"

"Opa asked me to stay. He'll pay me to live with him."

"Wish my mom would do the same. So what do you want? Too bored with yourself? No pussy to chase?"

"I had a lot going on."

"Yeah, you got a new car, not that I would know, because you haven't even showed me yet."

"You want a ride?"

He thought about that, grinned, said, "Not really. I mean, not now anyway."

"I'm sorry." Not because I felt it, but because I felt it was necessary.

"Right," he said. "So what do you want?"

"Do you think I should stay with Opa?" I said.

He shrugged. "Do you have a choice? I mean, even if Julie's parents let you stay, that costs money, and who is going to pay for it? Unless, of course, you get a job." He paused for a moment. "You don't like him?"

"He says we're cut from the same cloth."

"What does that mean?"

"He says we keep to ourselves, don't have many friends, don't trust anyone but family. That sort of thing."

Miles nodded. "Do you agree?"

"I'm afraid of that."

"How?"

"Have you ever talked to my grandpa? He saved me when Mark came over to kill me, but when we're alone, I don't know, it's like somebody is there in the room with you, but you can't be sure who it is. Like with bears. I once read that no matter how they feel, they don't betray it in their facial expressions. You can't tell if it wants to be petted or if it's going to kill you."

"He's a doctor. He's not supposed to harm anyone."

"I didn't say he'd harm anyone."

"Except for Mark."

"Except for Mark."

After that we were silent, and the room felt emptier now, as though I had enough space to sit and rest for a while. I told myself that Miles was an animal with a certain particular smell. And so was I. We weren't close, not the way Katia and I had been, and yet we had always known each other.

"So you're going to stay?" he finally asked.

"He's got cancer," I said. "Leukemia. Says he'll be fine but wants my help when he seeks treatment."

"Shit," Miles said. "How bad is it?"

I shrugged. "He's getting loopy. Like he's forgetting who he is. Ever since he beat up Mark. He didn't have a scratch, not a single scratch." Before Miles could ask me another question, I said, "What are you going to do after the summer? Are you leaving for college?"

"College? Maybe. But I am going to leave, with the Sturdy Turds or by myself, I don't care. Can you imagine staying in this town, together with Mark and Julie and all the rest of them?"

I didn't answer him. Later, long after I had left, I kept chewing that question like gum, over and over, until the flavor was all gone. And the answer made me afraid, because yes, yes, I could imagine staying. Or better, I couldn't imagine any kind of life outside this town. No matter how much I hated it and how little it offered to me, what would I be without it?

Where was Katia? Why hadn't she given me her address? I kept the engine running, and it took me another hour before I dared enter Opa's house again.

•

On April 16th, the last snowstorm closed schools and stores because even our small town, where winter felt at home and so comfortable it followed us everywhere and returned even after we had thrown it out; even our small town owned only so many dependable snowplows. It was also the day Opa was supposed to appear in court. He was in a foul mood, and the foul weather made it worse. He wanted to go, he wanted to tell Mark, Skip, and Tony what he thought of them. He didn't see the need for an attorney. Opa Frank was indignant that Mark had gone to the police and that, backed by his parents' money, he'd pressed charges against him. The Sellers family had made a fortune in real estate, starting with the doomed convention center, and owned half the commercial buildings in town. But decency would easily defeat money, Opa said. Any idiot could see that he had just defended his grandson.

His office, in the meantime, had suffered. While to some

people he'd become a folk hero, many of his patients appeared to side with Mark—a doctor they'd trusted had attacked three boys with a weapon. Opa told me not to worry, but his steps had become more deliberate, as though he were pushing a heavy cart in front of him. Even in the mornings, while making toast and drinking coffee, he appeared to be lost in thought. He forgot things now, asked me the same thing twice within in a few minutes.

I offered to give him a ride, but he scoffed, "In that tin coffin? In this weather?" Instead, he got into his Lincoln, five sandbags in the trunk putting weight on the wheels. "We might have to walk home," he grumbled.

What followed once we had entered the county courthouse was not the grand affair I had expected. There were cases to be decided before ours. Fat men in jeans and winter boots sat on low benches along the walls, women with greasy hair tied tightly around their skulls kept them company while kids chased one another down the hallway. There was a vending machine for hot coffee, and after Opa had put a quarter in the slot, the machine burped, sputtered, and spit out hot water.

Mark, Skip, Tony, and their parents, were already sitting inside the courtroom, dressed to the nines. On another day, I would have laughed at Mark's red tie, today though, it frightened me. A scar ran across Mark's temple; his hair had been cut short to showcase it. I only wore a wool sweater and down coat, Opa Frank a light-blue sweater vest under a brown leather jacket. He was too proud for a hat.

By the time Opa was called in front of the judge, my back was sweaty, my face hot. After his initial testimony, which he delivered in a dry, measured voice, Mark's family's lawyer, someone from Bay City, peppered him with questions. Had Mark been armed? Why was Opa keeping a bat in his car? Did he know what excessive force meant?

"I know a coward when I see one," Opa said. "Three against one. Who do you think was using excessive force?"

But the lawyer didn't stop. Did Opa have anger issues? Why hadn't he called the police? Why had he taken matters into his own hands?

Opa Frank's face was as red as I imagined mine to be. "Three against one," he said once more. "And that one"—he pointed at me—"is my only grandson. Yes, I am a grandfather, and I have the right to protect the ones I love, and these little scumbags in their suits and ties can call themselves lucky I only kept a bat in my trunk."

Of course I was called as a witness. Of course I told everyone exactly what had happened. But the lawyer made more of me sleeping with Mark's girlfriend than of Mark driving up to my house. The horrible thing was that the longer the lawyer talked, the more I believed his story. Opa and I looked like hooligans out to hurt people. The longer I listened to Mark's testimony, the more I despised myself and Opa. What we had done was no different than robbing small children of their lunch money or making fun of the disabled.

Opa, representing himself, asked questions too. But by then, his carefully combed hair was in disarray, his voice loud and harsh. He asked Mark if he was dealing weed, and, when that question was disallowed, asked if he was taking drugs. That question was disallowed too, and it rattled Opa. He hadn't pre-pared well—the case had been so clear. And when it was finally over, he had lost. Anger management classes and dozens of hours of community service, plus payment of Mark's family lawyer's costs.

Opa turned first to me, as though he hadn't heard the ver-dict, then turned toward the spectators, wordless, seeing and understanding nothing.

Julie stood in one of the back rows, in a green dress. She is waiting for me, I thought for a second in which my heart seemed to swell and burst in a cartoonish way. She wore sandals, her toes were painted the same green color as her dress. Sandals in a snowstorm—I wanted to take my coat and wrap her pudgy feet. She's waiting for me. I'm here, I have been waiting for you as well. I have been waiting for weeks. She hadn't spotted me yet, and like an idiot I raised my hand. She waved too, but her eyes hadn't even detected me. She was there for Mark, who now strode quickly toward her. She put her arms around his waist, and they were a lovely couple, so well-matched.

"Let's go home," Opa said in my back, and I put my arm around his shoulders and led him from the courtroom. He handed me the car keys without a word, got out from under my grasp and trudged toward the exit. "Not that way," I said. "We're parked out front." I had to repeat myself—people were coming and going, people in fur coats and cheap plastic jackets, with soda cups from Fancy's and strollers. Finally he stopped, turned around, and walked right past me. I followed at a little distance.

He didn't say anything during the ride home, nor did he talk once I had unlocked the front door. He walked up the stairs, closed his bedroom door, and I didn't see him again until later that night, when I was sitting in the kitchen reading about war planes in an old magazine.

•

He was wearing pajamas and a robe, his feet stuck in fur slippers. Opening the refrigerator, he reached for a large kielbasa sausage, grabbed two beers and put one in front of me. He started to eat even before he'd sat down, and we didn't speak until the whole sausage was gone. He gave off a lubricant odor.

"What if my daughter suffered an accident that turned her into not-Maggie?"

I remember his eager face, the swollen veins on his forehead. He had lost his mind. "What?" I shook my head as if my thoughts were flies swarming my mind. I needed them gone to make room for whatever monstrosity was to come from Opa Frank's lips.

"What if she had lost her ability to cope with the world? What if she became too afraid to set foot into the world?"

You don't need to be asleep to have nightmares. A broken foot needs a cast, but what had happened to Opa? What had been broken inside his head that morning in the courtroom? Who would I call for help? There was no one left in my family; Uncle Bobby hadn't visited in over ten years. I didn't even have his number. "Afraid of what?"

He didn't listen, he wasn't done yet outlining his scenario. "What if she'd become pregnant? Paul was a grown man and knew his way around women. Of course they did it, and she was with child."

"But she ran off."

"What if she didn't?"

"Run off?"

"What if she wanted to stay, but this man wouldn't let her? What if he stalked her? What if he waited in front of her home trying to intimidate her? What if he made her lose her mind, and she needed shelter from him? What if she needed to disappear *and* stay? Stay where she was safe and disappear so she wouldn't be dragged away by someone who would surely hurt her?"

"But she did leave with him," I said after he'd fallen silent. "They lived together until she left for California."

Opa Frank inhaled as though he'd been under water for a long time. "Yes, she did. But what if she hadn't?"

"She'd be sitting here with us?" I said. "She'd be about Mom's age and her kids would be my age?"

"Yes," Opa said. "Yes. Now you make sense of the scenario."

"What scenario?"

He took off his glasses and looked at me with eyes that seemed blind and unable to recognize anything beyond his hands on the table in front of him.

"You okay?" I asked. "I know you must miss her a lot." I didn't know, I hadn't lost a daughter and not seen her for decades. I hadn't driven anyone away. I had never hired a detective in vain. But it was something that felt safe to say. "Maybe Paul finds her this time. Maybe he finds her, and they let us know they're safe."

Opa Frank nodded, though his gaze didn't change. His eyes were pebbles, smooth and useless. "Let's pray she's safe."

"Why wouldn't she be?"

He looked at me for several seconds, maybe a minute. I held my breath; whatever he said next would certainly drown me.

"Paul was not a good man."

"Was?"

"When they met. Few people change."

"But you said…"

"I took pity on him and bought his car. I did it for her. For Maggie."

"So he could go find her."

"What?" He looked startled. "Today…it's not your fault, but today I realized that I won't always be here. Let me correct myself. I have always known. I'm a sick man. I won't last forever, but today—what if they had arrested me?"

"They wouldn't arrest you."

"I'd be gone and what would happen here?"

"I'm here," I assured him. "I'd hire a lawyer for you. I'm not a kid anymore."

"But you don't know," he said in a strange voice. This wasn't an accusation but a lament. "You have no eyes or ears. You haven't pieced together what is going on around you. And this is also not your fault. I've been meticulous, I know how to protect the ones I love."

I went to the refrigerator for more beer. Whatever had happened in the courtroom, it had deflated Opa, maybe defeated him. This is the day, I thought, a fork in the road, a turning point. At his funeral, I'll remember this day. I set another beer in front of him.

"It's time," Opa said. "I knew what I was asking of you when I requested you stay another year, though I thought I would have more time to prepare you. Let's go."

"In this weather? Where are we going?"

He grabbed my arm, pulled me up. "You won't need a jacket."

7

What does it take to mutilate someone? What would it take to make it feel justified? How would you explain it to the ones around you? What frame would you build, what color would you paint it to give that explanation life? What does it take to kill another person?

There was a moment of success in my life, many years later, when critics and collectors called my work "understated, yet daring" and detected a "quiet terror" one could almost overlook, it appeared so casual.

My pictures haven't changed much, but the market has moved on. During that moment when personal history and artistic ambition overlapped, critics wanted to entice the market. For two years it appeared to work, then the focus shifted. Interest turned into distaste, what was wrong with me? Why was I holding on to my past? How could I expect collectors to pay for the sins of the past? Did they really want my portraits and figures in their hallways? In their living-rooms? In their bedroom? After they'd learned the history of my paintings?

The market moved on once collectors sensed that I didn't have a prepared narrative. And why didn't I have one? Why hadn't I rushed to prepare one? One that explained why I stayed with Opa even after that last winter night in April?

·

I didn't need a jacket, because Opa took me to the basement. From one of his pockets he produced a key and instead of walking into his 'museum,' he unlocked a door that I had never noticed before and that didn't seem to be a door at all, so neatly did it fit into the wood-paneled wall. The effect was achieved largely because the paneling was imperfect, the grooves a bit crooked, the wood rough—treated, not painted. It appeared to be the work of a talented and inexperienced amateur.

I stood behind my grandfather and laughed, because I feared being stuck with him in the basement. I knew what Opa could do to three guys, and what if he decided to beat me and lock me up down here so I would stay another year in his house? Does it feel like hindsight, this feeling of foreboding and distrust? It might, but I do remember how I laughed because I didn't know what to say. Then the door swung open, and I could see that it was made from thick metal, like the backdoors on industrial buildings, fire doors. This one was soundproofed. The wood had only been applied to the outside to hide its existence.

She did not look like Mom. I had seen her before, though she'd been wearing shiny pumps and a thin coat in the snow-storm. Her hair wasn't wet this time, but beautifully long and soft. Her face wasn't pretty, not the way Julie and Katia were pretty, though her lips were still full. Her round belly and sloped shoulders made her look ashamed and benevolent, like someone who was afraid of you or pitied you and couldn't wait to give you a hug and make you some hot tea. Her chin was small, she could tuck it into her neck. She hugged Opa, pulled him close, and after she had released him, she looked at me and said, "You're Carol's son." And she opened her arms once more, and I was too stricken to refuse. Crickets nested in my ears. I couldn't feel a thing.

Opa closed and locked the door behind us. "Don't want anyone to intrude," he said.

"I saw you," I said, because there wasn't anything else to say. "Years ago."

Maggie stared at me, open-eyed and faced, only squinting after a second, cocking her head just to let me know she was thinking about where that might have been.

"Nonsense," Opa said. "Where is everybody?"

"They're napping," she said.

I looked from one to the other. The crickets became louder, echoes upon echoes, and I noticed that the room we were standing in had no windows. It was a cozy room and smelled faintly of patchouli, a smell Rebecca had taught me, and neither Maggie nor Opa Frank answered my stare. Opa took Maggie's hand, squeezed it, and said. "Go get them. I want them to meet their cousin."

A minute or two later, a giant shape was released from the dusk of the adjoining room. It ducked its head; the doorframe wasn't tall enough. "He's two years your junior. Smart as a whip." Opa stood next to the boy now, beaming. "Greg, this is your cousin," he said.

"Hi." Greg stretched out a fat hand. His eyes were almost white and squinting, as though he'd never been outside and had never experienced sunlight.

Sometimes I come close to imagine what death feels like. In the moment my hand disappeared in his, my whole body puckered because I understood, in that one instant, that Greg had never set foot outside.

"And here's my sweetheart." Opa Frank reached behind him and pulled a very pale girl into the room, then rested his hands on her white shoulders. She was wearing a wifebeater and gym pants, no bra. These are the things you shouldn't notice first, but I did. Not for an instant did I believe it was Katia and still, I forgot to breathe. The similarities were so glaring. This girl was beautiful in a lazy way, the drawing of Katia by someone who was a bit tired or just in a generous mood. Long black hair curled about her face, a face that belonged to my sister but was fuller. Like Greg, she too had very light, silvery eyes. "Give your cousin a hug," Opa said to the girl. "This is Frances. Franny."

The girl stepped forward and slung her arms around my neck. She pulled me close, the way Maggie had pulled in Opa Frank, and for the briefest of moments, I let myself be overwhelmed by the familiarity. Somehow, Katia had been returned to me.

"Franny is fifteen, a young lady." Opa sounded prouder than I'd ever heard him. The girl kissed me on the lips and said, "Hey you."

I waited for someone to explain the situation to me, to come up with a story I could believe, a tale that would convince me that the basement I stood in was something different than it appeared to be. There would be an explanation that conformed to a world I was familiar with. Still, with a clarity that hurt my stomach and made my chest cave in, I knew that no such thing was to follow. It was, above all things, simple. This was Opa's family. They had always lived here. My whole life.

My face must have said as much. Everybody was quiet, though not concerned. They gave me time to recover, they were being polite. A moment later, Maggie started to make coffee. "We need more sugar soon."

Frances took my hand, squeezed it, and pulled me toward a chair. "It'll only be a moment," she said. "You're much taller than I imagined. Almost as tall as Greg."

Greg grunted behind me. I sat at the small wooden table in what appeared to be the kitchen. I looked around, I did not remember ever seeing any of the furnishings, and I knew without thinking about it, that none of these things had been appropriated from the upstairs. These had been bought new, for the purpose of being used in this apartment under Opa's house.

"Give him a tour, Franny." Opa took a seat at the table. "Come on, girl."

Frances reached for my hand again. "I'll show you," she said, "though, if we'd known you'd come to see us, I would have cleaned up."

"She's very tidy." Maggie set the table while keeping an eye on us. "Don't believe a word she says."

Frances pulled. I tried to adjust my steps, avoid contact, but I had to duck under the door to enter the next room, and she stopped abruptly. "Oops," she said. "This is our living room, I guess." It contained a small sofa and two armchairs, a coffee table taken over by a record-player and thirty or forty albums. The room was carpeted in an oily beige. Light came through a window that didn't open and looked out onto a shaft. Franny caught me staring at it and put an arm around my waist. "It's dark most of the time, but we have each other and we have Frank. Family is always first, don't you think? And now I have you, too."

There were two more rooms. The first one was shared by Franny and Greg, their beds on opposite ends. The last one held a much larger bed and belonged to Maggie. "But we can only take a peek," Franny said before closing the door again. "Mom's very strict. It's her own room. Frank's too, but only when he visits."

She sat down on her bed, on a pinkish comforter with farm animals printed on the material. She patted the space next to her.

"I'm okay," I said.

"You don't have to be afraid. I'm not."

"I'm not afraid," I protested.

"Frank said you would be. It's a lot to take in."

There was a small bookshelf close to her bed. I walked up to the rows of books, tried to read their titles in the twilight of the bedroom. "You like horses?" I said.

"Not anymore. That's for younger girls. Greg is reading them now."

I nodded without comprehending. "What are you reading these days?"

"Mom gave me *Madame Bovary*, but she's such a bore. I tried *To the Lighthouse* but it's unreadable. I prefer Hemingway and Edgar Allen Poe. Especially Poe."

I looked at the spines in order not to glance her way. Too closely did her face resemble my sister's. I liked her voice, which was flat and pleasant. It possessed no real quality you could describe. Only her pronunciation was odd, as though she'd immigrated from somewhere else, a land made of right angles, all tiled, with men sporting mustaches and women chromed boots.

"I think the coffee is probably ready," I said.

"They're not expecting us anytime soon."

"What do you mean?" I was still not looking in her direction, only read the sounds that came from her bed. Of course, Opa had always known how much Katia and Frances looked alike; it appeared obvious that he had anticipated my confusion, my greed. He'd carefully set his trap. "I'd like some coffee." My voice was barely audible, and I didn't wait for Frances to follow.

The kitchen turned out to be the largest room. Returning to the others, I could see a washer and dryer unit in one corner. Another door, half open, led to what appeared to be a bathroom. Green tiles. Sea foam.

"I need to go," I was shaking, and Opa didn't hesitate to reach into his pocket and hand me the keys. "Take it slow," he said. "I trust you, son."

Nobody stopped me after I had unlocked the entrance. Neither Greg, Frances, nor Maggie, tried to push me aside and run toward the stairs leading up to Opa's house. Before I pushed the heavy door shut again, I stood for a brief moment and took in the four people gathered around the kitchen table. Not even Frances glanced my way. They were drinking coffee and eating scones from a large earthen bowl.

•

He arrived late, though I knew he would want to speak to me. I sat on the bed, headphones on. The music didn't help me understand a thing, but the volume was turned up high and kept my thoughts from straying past that wall of noise. Given the chance, they would surely bare their teeth and attack. I kept my body still, even after Opa Frank sat down near my feet. Had he touched me, I swear, I would have run.

"They are your family, too," he repeated after I had taken off the headphones. The music kept playing; I was too afraid to switch it off.

"I don't know them," I said. "I don't know you."

He nodded, kept silent. He took off his glasses to wipe at them.

"She never left," I said.

He replaced the glasses, as though he needed them to speak. "No, she never did. She would have suffered unnecessarily."

"Who is Greg's father?" The darkness of my room was left incomplete by the lights along our streets and my stereo's display. The man at the foot of my bed was made from smoke, shifting, dissolving, entering my nostrils. He couldn't be contained. "It can't be Paul. It can't be."

"It isn't," my grandfather said. "He's mine." Then, "She'd always wanted children."

I pulled my legs up, away from him. I made myself as small as I could. "You've kept her imprisoned. She wanted to marry Paul. She wanted to leave. She just wanted to get out of this town and away from you." I thought these words would eviscerate him or make him attack me. In hindsight, I know that he only heard what he expected. He heard what he himself knew to be true.

"I was selfish," he said after a long silence. "My love for her is too big. Much too big. I love her more than I have ever loved anyone. Your sister, your mother and uncle—I would give up all of you before I let someone like Paul take away my Maggie."

He didn't raise his voice, nor did he try to touch me while I covered my face and cried. I was thinking of Katia and wished for her to see me and hold me, and I didn't even know her address. I didn't have anyone. Not Julie, not Rebecca, not even Mom or Dad. When I was done crying and opened my eyes again, Opa was gone.

•

In the morning, I moved my dresser away from the door. The daylight was the color of dishwater, my bag packed. I might not finish school, but I wasn't worried about grades and diploma. I'd go to the police, then drive to New York to find my sister. I knew where home was. Wherever Katia was living now, that's where I needed to be.

I didn't care to know whether Opa Frank was home or not, whether he was in the basement or in his bedroom. Last night I had contemplated jumping from my window, but I needed him to know that I wasn't afraid. All these were helpless gestures, and yet I needed them to prop myself up, when all I wanted was darkness. I wanted to float into a world where there was no family, no town, no court, no Maggie, no Frances, no me.

My very first memory of Opa Frank was of him driving my father's red coupe. Now I realized that Greg had already been born, Maggie had already been living for years in the basement. My history felt rearranged. Opa's lies were not new, had kept his second family hidden even then.

The temperature had risen, and slush filled the streets. The large heaps of old snow that plows had built over the long winter had begun to melt. The car wouldn't start, and even before Opa Frank had reached the Pontiac, I knew he was the reason why the engine wouldn't come alive. I grabbed my bag from the passenger seat, got out, and started to walk away.

"Don't," Opa Frank called after me. "Just hear me out."

I kept walking. Icy water was ruining my shoes; my feet were already soaked.

"One hour. Just one hour. Then drive off. I won't keep you."

"One hour?"

He was holding the spark plugs in his hand. "Just come inside."

"I'll call the police," I said.

"That's up to you."

"You don't think I'm going to," I said.

"I'm seventy years old. I've had my share. It's you I'm worried about."

There are moments in life that afterwards, when you look at them from a distance of years and thousands of miles, appear to have been very simple. There was only one good choice, and it was easy to see, you recognize. And yet, you couldn't find it. It was right there in front of you, but you missed a step, you faltered when just another step would have delivered you. People ask why you didn't see that next step, why you turned another way, and you shrug, you can't answer that question. You just can't. What you felt back then is hidden from you, the way you forget why you stopped running during the last miles of a marathon. No pain is insurmountable, you want to say, another push and you could have managed, you were so close. But back then, I couldn't see and feel anything. Back then, my feet were freezing and wet. My car wouldn't take me to Katia.

We sat down in the kitchen, and Opa cooked breakfast, bacon and eggs. This was extravagant by his standards, but he handled himself with the efficiency of a short-order cook. It was a workday, yet here he was in an old sweater and slacks and house shoes.

"Thank you," he said when he put the plate of food in front of me. The spark plugs lay at the center of the table. "We should have talked last night, but you seemed distraught."

"You're a freak," I said. "Maggie is your daughter. Your daughter. Daughter." My voice jumped high, where no air was left.

"Yes, yes she is. And I want to keep protecting her."

"It's a prison. You're not protecting her. Nobody would do anything to harm them. It's you, it's you who is harming her."

Would he take the pan and hit me? Would he burn my face with the hot grease? But no, Opa Frank kept his hands and face in check. "I want to die here, not in prison," he said flatly. "But I'm not afraid for myself. Imagine you walk into the police station today and tell the cops."

"Did you stay up all night to watch what I was doing?"

"There was no need."

"Because you had the plugs."

"Because you're stronger than you know but about as far away from knowing your own potential as Mars is away from

Earth. One day, you'll put it all together, but it took your mom fifty years before she knew she wanted to help people in far-flung places, and I can't wait for you to come to your senses. It's simple. I won't last forever, and my family needs to prepare for a time when I won't be able to take care of them."

"So let them go."

"It's not that easy."

"Because you'd go to jail."

"Because they've never lived outside of this house. Imagine you go to the cops. They'll take them away from me, put me in prison. How are Maggie, Franny, and Greg, going to take care of themselves? I'm not poor, but I don't have savings. They'd run out of money in no time, and then what?"

"They can sell the house, they can sell their story to the newspapers, they can work. Greg can work, Frances can work. They're not crippled." I didn't want to, but I ate. The bacon sickened me, but I stuffed my face with everything Opa had cooked. I was leaving, I had made up my mind. The cops could sort out this mess; it wasn't my fault.

"If you talk to the cops today, don't count on leaving anytime soon. I won't blame you. I will tell them what I did and how I did it, but they won't believe you weren't in on it." He said that casually, no threat hoarsened his voice. "If you leave now, how do you explain you didn't know about the basement? You won't see Katia again for a while. That's where you're going, isn't it? New York."

"Shut up."

"You have a second choice. You finish high school in six or seven weeks, then you get into that car and leave for New York. You'll never have to see me or any of us again. Forget about us if you can. If I die, it's not your responsibility. Nobody will ever find out what happened here."

"But if you die, they'll die too."

"What's in me is also inside of you. We're cut from the same cloth. We both love who we're not supposed to. You and I, we know how it feels to love the one person we mustn't touch. But that didn't keep me. It didn't keep you."

"I didn't lock her up."

"You packed your bag to go see her. You think I don't know how you lived together next door, sleeping in your parents' bed like a married couple? You think I didn't see the way you looked at each other? And why didn't I say a thing? Why didn't I write a letter to your mom, asking her to come back?"

"Why?" My voice was only a whisper.

"Because I understood. I'm a monster, but I never tried to be. I tried to lead a decent life, and couldn't. You can't either. It's not your fault you were made that way. You love your sister, you would do anything for her." He sat down at the table opposite of me, cut his bacon and ate. He poured himself a second cup of coffee. "Franny is beautiful. She hasn't had a boyfriend yet."

I grabbed the spark plugs, put them in the pocket of my hoodie. "I'm leaving now."

"She'll lose everything. Her family, her home. Everything."

I rose and walked toward the front door. I pulled another pair of socks from my bag, slipped into another pair of shoes. Opa Frank didn't come after me. The door slammed shut behind me, and I avoided the deepest puddles. I popped the hood and after five minutes, I sat behind the wheel. I expected flat tires, an engine fire, but by the time I sat idling in front of the Sheriff's office, no warning lights had come on, the motor was purring, the cabin was warm. Two cruisers stood parked out front. The sun was finally peeking through the clouds.

8

Opa didn't thank me, he was smarter than that. He didn't mention I had been gone for hours. No light was left in the sky, and on my way up the porch steps I told myself it was the courageous thing to do. The right thing. Ratting out family to the police was sacrilege, unthinkable. Instead, I needed to sort things out myself and make sure Maggie and her family were freed and wouldn't be separated.

He waited for me inside the kitchen, over a glass of brandy. He didn't look relieved, didn't smile. I didn't sit down at the table with him. Standing by the sink, I gave him an ultimatum. He would give them money; we could find them jobs. I had the upper hand now, I told myself. I would use it for good. We shook hands on it, solemnly. I demanded to see Maggie at once.

"It's late, they're asleep," he said softly. "We'll do it first thing in the morning."

"First thing." During the night I dreamed that Katia had returned. She was much older now, as old as Mom, but I knew it was her, and she hugged me, and deep happiness flooded me. I meant to smell her skin; it was made from cookie dough.

•

In the morning, he was nowhere to be found. It was only half past six when I stepped into the kitchen, fully dressed. At first, I expected him to be in the basement, preparing Maggie and her children for the changes I was going to impose, but while I was brewing coffee I saw that the Lincoln had left the driveway.

Moments later, the doorbell rang. It's the cops, I thought, Opa finally confessed. They're here to free Maggie and put me in handcuffs. The Grand Prix stood parked curbside. If I left the house through the side door, maybe I could get away unseen. I could make it to Detroit by afternoon.

Rebecca's hair was dyed black and short, she looked skinnier than she'd ever been. "Where's Katia?" was the first thing that came to my mind. I stepped out onto the porch, looking for Ingri's old Cadillac or any car with New York license plates, my sister in the passenger seat. I had dreamed of her; she was here to see me, here to stay.

Rebecca shrugged. "It's just me. Can I come in?"

Maggie and her kids were holed up in the basement waiting for Opa or me to come and provide them with food and company. If I wanted to free them, this was the moment. Rebecca and I only had to force open the door. "Sure," I said. "I guess."

"You're weird," she said. "Anything the matter?"

"No, come in. My grandpa isn't here."

"Is that important?"

"It's not even seven yet. What do you want?" I turned away from her and walked back toward my bedroom. The packed bag sat on my desk chair. Rebecca looked at it, raised her eyebrows, then took a seat on the floor. She wore black socks, black pants, and a ratty black wool sweater so full of holes you could see her bra. I plopped down on my bed and pulled the covers tight around me.

"Where are you going?" she said.

"Just came back."

"During the school year?"

"Why are you here?"

"It's not like I broke your heart," she said. "How's that Julie thing going?"

"Why are you here?" I wondered if Maggie could hear the floorboards creak. For the first time I wondered if she kept track of the comings and goings of everyone in the house. Had she listened to her mother clean the house? Had she tried to bang against pipes to let her know she lived hidden away in the basement?

"I need you to come to a funeral with me. Ingri is dead. That's why I'm here. I'm leaving again in two days. But you're the only one who got to know her, and I'm not going by myself."

"Your parents will be there."

"I'm not staying with my parents."

"You just arrived?"

"I just arrived."

"And you need a place to stay?"

"It's seven o'clock in the morning."

"You don't even like me."

"But at least you don't hate me."

I stared at the door to my room. I listened for Opa's Lincoln, I listened for any noise coming from the basement. "It's not a good time," I said.

Rebecca laughed. "No shit." She kept laughing until I was finally laughing too.

"It's horrible." I was glad she didn't even know what I was referring to.

"I haven't been able to hold down a job," she said. "I can't make it work. I start, everybody seems happy with what I'm doing at first, and then I get into an argument with a customer, and that woman was a cunt, believe me, but they blame me for it. One guy who hired me told me after three days that I was too sullen. I asked him what that meant, and he just says, 'You're dull, no spirit.'"

"Where's your shit?"

"On the front porch. I didn't want…I hitchhiked up here. I would have come yesterday, but some prick dropped me off in the middle of nowhere because I didn't like his hand rubbing my thigh. I really thought about letting him do that shit because he would have driven me all the way up here, but he wasn't even…never mind."

"You can stay here," I said. "I'll let Opa know. I'll get your shit."

On my way to the front door, I tried to see my way forward, try to imagine a way to work Rebecca into my plans of freeing Maggie without getting Opa arrested. What if I told Rebecca about the family living in the basement? What would she do? Would she run? Go to the cops? Would she still want to stay?

Her bag was small, a brown fake-leather thing, the material rubbed bare in patches, the strap mended. For a second, I saw myself luring Rebecca to the basement, pushing her into Maggie's apartment and locking the door behind her. I suddenly hated her, and the hatred made me clench my jaw and quicken my steps. I pushed the door to my room open, ready to scream at her for abandoning Katia and having the gall to come to my door. I needed to throw her out.

She was asleep on the floor. My entrance only roused her enough so I could help her into my bed. "You need to wake me up at three. The funeral is at four." I said I would, and she went immediately back to sleep. Her breath stank.

I waited in the kitchen and by half past nine, Opa Frank was back. He nodded his head while I was telling him about Rebecca. He'd bought groceries—milk, sugar, hot dogs, sauerkraut, mustard, rice pudding—and while he unpacked the things he intended to keep for himself, he said, "It's a change of plan."

"Not a change," I insisted. "We're just postponing."

Three shopping bags remained on the kitchen counter. "You want to take them downstairs?" he asked.

It was that question that tore through my stupor. It was no longer only my grandfather who was keeping Maggie hostage. We were doing it together. By not going to the police immediately I had become his accomplice. The next second, I had rearranged my thoughts. No, I was the reason they would be freed. I was the reason why Maggie and her kids stood a chance against Opa Frank. "Okay," I said.

•

Nobody was in the kitchen. Music was playing at low volume—how Opa Frank had kept Maggie hidden from his wife? His was such a staggering project. A living installation, breathing, moving, changing with the birth of his children. This part of the basement had started as maybe a small room, a storage space next to Opa's museum, which took up most of the original basement. And over the years he had dug his way past the foundation and deep into the backyard. Had Oma Anna been in on it? Had she agreed to keep Maggie imprisoned? Constructing an entire basement apartment was such an arduous, noisy, filthy task, she must have known, I thought, and sought to reconcile Oma's good cheer and cookies with her watching Opa emerge from the basement with dark soil under his nails. How had he explained the excavated dirt? How had he carried in the building materials without his wife knowing what they were meant for? They'd been married for forty years. How did you keep three prisoners a secret? Had Oma Anna cooked for them?

This was the first time I suspected my grandmother, and my thoughts didn't stop there. If Oma Anna had known the truth about Maggie and her children, was it possible that Mom had found out and kept quiet as well? Were Katia and I the only ones not in on the scheme? Was Maggie's imprisonment the reason why Mom had left town again?

But when had she found out? Before or after she had moved into the house next door? Had she blackmailed Opa into giving her the down payment? And was that why Opa almost never came to visit us? Why he hadn't tried to keep her around?

I stood in that low-ceilinged kitchen, grocery bags in hand, and I couldn't move. Everybody had been in on it, everybody had known. It couldn't be any other way. You couldn't store away a whole family in a basement without people above finding out about it. The toilet flushing, a kid crying at night, Greg listening to music—you couldn't keep a secret like that. It was impossible.

Was it, though? I had lived for several months upstairs without suspecting anything. Julie and I had made love while Maggie and Greg and Frances were living separated by just the floorboards.

I put down the bags, stretched out an arm to touch that ceiling. I knocked. Could someone above hear the sound? Or had Opa soundproofed Maggie's prison? Had he worked every weekend to make sure his family stayed undetected?

"Hello? Oh hey!" It was Frances, beaming. She wore the same sweatpants I'd seen her in the last time, and just a bra, some lacy thing that looked as stiff as cardboard. "We're having breakfast in the living room." Then her eyes caught sight of the bags and she yelped and grabbed the first one and carried it to the kitchen table. I watched her rifle through the bags, then pull out items and inspect them. "He won't buy chocolate. Not ever. He says it will fatten us too much."

"Really?" I asked stupidly. Her shoulders were a bit rounded, her skin white as soap. But when she lifted a package of raisins and turned it in her hand, she became Katia.

"Will you buy me some chocolate next time?"

"Next time? Next time you might buy chocolate yourself."

She wheeled around to face me. Her bra didn't move, and she must have seen that I was studying her. "What do you mean?" Her teeth were yellow, small. And all of a sudden, I grew aware that I didn't understand the first thing about this girl. How was she able to walk and hold herself up when she had never left the basement? "Are you taking me somewhere?"

But I never got to answer her, because Maggie entered the kitchen, a smile forming and falling away. "Is Frank okay? Why is he sending you?"

"He said I can buy chocolate myself next time," Frances said, not waiting for my answer.

"What's going on?" Maggie's face was wrinkled. Mom had never shown me a photograph of her sister, nor had Maggie appeared in any of the pictures Oma Anna dusted meticulously every week. The topic of her eldest child was taboo in Opa's house.

I listened to my aunt without hearing a word, without answering any of her questions. I was overwhelmed by the feeling that nobody I had ever lived with I'd come to know.

Nobody had cared enough to reveal what they thought, felt, or intended to do. Nobody had confided in me. And maybe, when you looked at the matter closely, there wasn't a whole lot of me there. Who was I? A boy who had made love to his sister, whose ex-girlfriend was sleeping upstairs in his bed even though she didn't care one bit about him. A boy whose aunt, the aunt he'd never seen, stood in front of him, still talking. He had just carried the groceries downstairs and caught himself staring at her daughter's white shoulders.

"What is it?" Maggie said.

Instead of answering, I ran. I locked the door behind me. I would forget about this, I needed to forget about this. I needed to leave for New York and find Katia. Katia would put her hands around my face and say, "Hey beautiful," and I would know that I really existed, that there was a me in this world, and that the world was more than people telling lies and keeping secrets, more than just pictures moving before my eyes.

When I got back upstairs, it was only Opa Frank eating toast in the kitchen. "How is everybody?" he said.

"I need to go to a funeral. Later. This afternoon. Rebecca will only stay for two days. How are we going to...have you ever taken them outside?"

He sipped some coffee to wash down the toast. "I wanted to. I thought about it. The only time I did, she nearly got away." His tongue searched his teeth for crumbs, then he took another bite of his toast, another sip of coffee. His hair was clean white, not of the yellow shade you saw in so many old people. His jawline was impressive, unlike Maggie's, Mom's, or my own. We had inherited Oma Anna's chin. Behind his glasses, his enlarged eyes were alive and clear.

"You should have told me about the cancer earlier," I said.

"There was no need for you to know. I've only known for the past two months myself."

"What are you going to do?"

"Maggie will receive everything except for the money that

goes to you. It will last you a while. I can show you the will. I have sinned. I have gravely sinned, but please, please, give me the time to make things right."

•

It was raining by the time we arrived at the cemetery. Everybody, it seemed, owned a new black car, everybody wore black clothes as though they had recently been purchased. There was an inner circle of what I took to be relatives, maybe friends from the time before Ingri had secluded herself. Those were bent figures, with faces that had lost contours and turned into something neither male nor female. The bodies wanted to shed their skin. Among these people of the inner circle, the expressions were grim or that of consternation, as though they couldn't understand what had happened. They were scared by their own incomprehension. Rebecca's parents, who I had previously seen around town but never met before, were the youngest, steadying their elders, pushing them into the right direction, toward the chapel.

The outer circle consisted of middle-aged people, no doubt friends and relatives of the Karvonens, maybe a few relatives who'd made the drive from a nearby town. I knew a few of them—Pete Saeger, the owner of the hardware store, Bob Svensen, who ran the local laundry service—but most of their faces, though vaguely familiar, I couldn't place. The men wore suits, the women extravagant dresses which were too new and shiny for the occasion. Their faces underneath black umbrellas showed mirth—Ingri's death provided them with an opportunity to get off work and socialize. The outer circle was louder, and they'd even brought a few kids. These were dressed with care but not in black; they hadn't received funeral clothes. A few played catch in the rain or hid between their parents' legs. The last ones to enter the chapel were Rebecca and I, each of us holding a white rose we'd bought in town. We hadn't thought of umbrellas; our hair and faces were full of water. Rebecca's make-up hadn't survived.

The casket stood open, but from where we stood in back, it was impossible to see Ingri. I wanted to advance, but Rebecca pulled me into a pew and told me to sit down. "Don't make a fuss."

The service was short. Becca's father said a few words in a voice that seemed to lip-sync sentences from a recording. The pastor told the story of young Ingri, daughter of immigrants, and how she had made her home in America and prospered. Next to me, Becca was shaking. When I pulled her close, she squirmed and pushed back angrily, but my unwanted attention finally seemed to calm her. It was easier to be furious with me than to feel sorrow for Ingri. The next moment her lips tickled my ear. "I hated her so much, but she was the only kind person in my family. She didn't understand how much I hated her, she was too stupid for that. In her world, somebody like me couldn't exist. So she thought I was nice."

Before the pastor had even ended, Rebecca stood to leave. I followed her outside, stole an umbrella from one of the racks. "What do we do now?" I asked in a low voice, even though the door had already closed behind us.

"We wait," she said.

We watched the funeral from inside my car, the windows rolled down because they wouldn't stop fogging up. I kept the engine running to blast hot air on our wet feet.

It was nearly dark before the last mourners had left and I woke Rebecca, whose flower lay crushed in her lap. "Shit," she said.

The casket had been lowered, but nobody had started to fill in the grave yet, except for the trowels of dirt the congregation had heaped on Ingri's casket. "Do you believe that she's some-where else?" Rebecca asked. "Somewhere different? Better?" She took the white rose from me, the last intact one, and threw it into the pit. "I hope she'll never have to meet me again."

"I hope there's no hell," I said. "I hope there's nothing, not even a thought. I hope that when I die, I will have left no trace, nothing. Like some weed in a desert."

"Weeds don't die," Becca said. "They multiply. Like rats and cockroaches."

"Then I want to be a unicorn. No unicorns left. Nothing."

"Don't make me laugh." She looked at the smashed rose she was still holding, shrugged, and threw it after the good one. "You're such an idiot. You're almost like a real person, but then you start talking, and it's this weird shit. You're all stunted, like you're some weird machine, some alien visitor, but they got the wiring all wrong. You're not a unicorn, you're a fucking moron."

"And why did you come to my house if I'm such a moron?"

"Shut up," Rebecca said. "You're ruining everything. Just stop talking." She sat down by the edge, legs dangling, then lowered herself into the grave. Face up, she lay on the casket, and rain ruined what little was left of her mascara. I walked back to my car, took off my soaked coat, sat staring at the rain running down my foggy windshield until she finally appeared and knocked on the side window. "I'm filthy," she said.

"Great. And?"

"You don't want to help a damsel in distress? You don't want to be my golden knight in rusty armor?" She wiggled her shoulders out of the coat, let it drop to the ground. "I'm getting really wet," she said, winking.

"Just get in," I said.

"No, you have to ask me. You have to ask me to get in."

"Get the fuck inside. Please!"

"The guy wasn't just rubbing my thighs the other night, you know. The one who dropped me by the side of the road?"

"Please?" I said. "Please get in."

"He offered me money. Seriously."

"Please get in. Becca, please!"

At home she showered, and I let her have some of my clothes, though she insisted they had to be gray or black. She wouldn't touch anything navy, or, god forbid, forest green. "You have no taste," she whined before she fell asleep in my bed. I had dinner by myself, dropping a bag of frozen beef pasta into a pot of boiling water and eating it without sauce. I ate the whole bag until I felt full, which is all I felt. Opa Frank was not in his room, but I didn't have the heart to even think about what that meant or what he might be doing in the basement. I gave myself a pass. I had Rebecca to worry about.

Black hairs were all over the shower, as though she had pulled out whole patches. I let the hot water run long after I was done rinsing. I still felt full, and now I was hot as well. I got into bed next to Rebecca. She'd used my cologne, the same cheap stuff I had bought for Katia years ago for Christmas. I lay on the outside, an inch from falling to the floor. I thought of Ingri's breasts floating in the bathwater. I thought of Katia wearing Dad's army coat. Rebecca slung an arm around me. "You can move closer. I'm not angry anymore. You're a beautiful unicorn," she murmured. "If only I were into you, everything would be fine."

•

"Some Finns are still doing it. Lapps, that is. Ingri told me when I was a little girl, but Dad said she was right." I had made breakfast, toast, jam, scrambled eggs. She stuffed herself, asked for more. After I filled a second thermos of coffee, she was in the mood to talk. She sat by the open window sipping coffee and smoking a cigarette.

"And how did they do it?" I asked.

"The reindeer would lie helpless on its back or side, with its head pressed against the ground and held down by one man's foot on the front branches of the antlers and a tight grip on the long main branches— to counteract the strength in the reindeer's neck. While one man held the bull, another got down on his knees behind it and put his hands and head between its back legs, grasped the testicles firmly between his fingers and bit off first one, and then the other. Ingri said they came off like a large gooseberry or a plum, one bite each, and then the pouch was massaged a little. Now the bull was an ox, was released, and trotted off to the other animals."

"Why would they do that? I mean, why wouldn't they take a knife?"

Rebecca shrugged. "Something about the reindeer still producing testosterone and breaking through the snow and ice to get to the vegetation. Dad couldn't remember. Or I don't remember."

"That's fucked up."

"I thought of that when the guy in the car offered me money. I thought, yes, pull down your pants, and I don't even have to hold your head down. You'll just be so happy I'm going to blow you, you'll let me do whatever I want down there. And I could suck in a ball or maybe both and bite them clean off." She lit another cigarette and stared at the low-hanging clouds, their undersides dirtied like cleaning rags.

"Did you do it?"

"What?"

"Bite his balls off."

"No, you moron. Otherwise I'd been here way earlier and would have some money."

"You're broke?"

"Can you drive me to town later?"

I looked at my watch, a cheap silver quartz thing. It was half past nine, there was no sense in trying to go to class. Biology. My teacher wore the thickest glasses I'd ever seen, his eyes invisible behind them. He was so short that he always raised his chin, always, and his arms and legs were thick. I couldn't remember what we had been working on last.

"Sure. What do you need to do?"

"Can I borrow some money from you?"

I gave her twenty dollars, most of what I had left, even though I would run out of gas soon. She still had that power over me. She could have asked anything of me that morning, and I would have made it happen.

"Why did you leave Katia?"

She didn't seem surprised at the question, though her lips grew thinner. "You ever been gone?"

"Sure."

"No, I mean have you ever lived outside of this shithole?"

"When I was little."

"You are one silly unicorn. You haven't seen anything, haven't felt anything. I know you guys love each other more than either of you has loved me. I get that. But just go someplace else, someplace bigger, and you might not even think about her anymore. What I'm trying to say is, it's like…have you ever read *The Little Prince* and the cheesy stuff about his one rose? That one rose he's got? And how it means so much to him, but if you had a field full of them, the one rose wouldn't be special at all?"

"What the hell?"

"Just listen. You're serving an old moan in a dry season. When we were all living here, Katia was very special. She wasn't like any of the other idiots here, present company included." She blew me a kiss. "But in New York, in New York nobody is like any of these idiots here in town. In New York she was the only one reminding me of this awful place."

"But you're back."

"Just because of Ingri."

"But you hated her."

"I won't be here for long."

The whole time I had been thinking about telling Rebecca the truth about Opa Frank. When she'd talked about the reindeer, I had been ready to take her to the basement, show her Opa's family. I wasn't sure what might happen if I unlocked the door, but I didn't need to know. Rebecca would make sense of the situation. As long as I took her to see Maggie, she would find a solution.

Yet I couldn't find that open space, that moment when I could steer the conversation to what was going on in this house. The more she spoke, the more remote she seemed, as though she had already left again. I poured us more coffee, bummed one of her cigarettes, and sat at the other window blowing smoke through the screen.

At two-thirty, we got in the car. The address was a lawyer's office in an old, slightly shabby, white Victorian. Two other cars stood in the graveled parking lot.

"Pick me up in an hour." She slung her large purse over one shoulder.

I didn't answer. She was already out the door, already on her way up the wooden stairs. I hadn't seen her so giddy since her arrival.

I parked in front of the hardware store and strolled through the aisles. Pete Saeger, the owner, recognized me and asked after Katia. I told him she was studying film at NYU, that she'd gotten a full ride and was doing great. I'd visit her in the summer; she'd just moved to her own apartment in the village.

He said he was very happy for her and hoped she would visit some time. His wife had just given birth to a little girl, and he was already saving for her college fund. I nodded, barely listened to his stories about his little daughter. Finally, he sauntered off and I was able to look for what I had come to buy. My last dollars bought me two packs of precision steel balls, and I dropped them into the back seat of the car.

•

At half past three, I returned to the lawyer's office. Only one car was still parked out front. I waited twenty minutes, then walked into the building. An older, heavy-set woman with a gray bun of hair asked what she could for me, and I told her I had come to pick up Rebecca.

"She has already left, I'm afraid," the woman said. "The meeting was very brief."

I drove through town, looking for Rebecca, the odd way she walked, as though her hips got in the way. I looked for her ratty coat, the short black hair. I drove a second time through town, then thought better of it and gunned the engine.

Opa hadn't returned yet, the front door was locked. Rebecca's bag was still under my desk, but when I opened it, only a few dirty pieces of clothing were left. Nothing of any value, no keys. She had been traveling lightly.

I told myself I wouldn't do it. Even when I arrived at the Karvonen's home, I was still telling myself I wouldn't. Minutes later I had rung the bell, and Mrs. Karvonen opened the door. I told her who I was, even blurted out that Becca had been staying with me. Was her daughter here? Could I see her?

Mrs. Karvonen's eyes welled up. She was still wearing black, something terribly stiff and simple. "She got what she wanted. She got what she came for." The voice didn't match the tears, was harsher, deeper than I had anticipated.

"She has already left?" I said. "How?"

"She was staying with you, not with us. You tell me." She dabbed at her eyes, but they were already dry again. "I guess she doesn't need you anymore either."

"Do you have an address for her?"

Mrs. Karvonen looked at me with some curiosity, as though I had performed a magic trick.

"The lawyer knows how to contact her. When they send her the inheritance, maybe they can insert a note that you are looking for her. Does she owe you money?"

"No," I said. "No."

"Well, then you're better off than most of her *friends*."

A voice became audible from the back of the house, and she turned and closed the door without looking at me or saying goodbye. I saw Ingri's casket again, Rebecca lying draped over it, and for a second, I could imagine what death would bring with it and how it would erase me swiftly and without giving me a thought. The next second, pain crowded my head, light stabbed my eyes. I walked down the footpath to my car. I would have to ask Opa for gas money.

9

Most of our thoughts are secondhand, we can't help it. We are conditioned by the language we learn as children, by the customs of our community, by the books we read, the newspapers we read, the movies we watch during workday matinees when you know you'll be one of only a few viewers and there's much space between each individual and the few couples that have ventured out and are scooting down in their seats. Yet a few moments in life might seem as though they belong to you. Not in any easy absolute way, but despite all the set-ups, despite of what you've learned, you never expected to find these moments. A moment like that might feel pleasurable or horrifying, and ideally it is both, and you know it's yours, yours alone. You live with the shame afterwards and still you mustn't lose sight of what you've done.

The first one of those came several months after our parents had left for the first time and Katia blindfolded me and asked me to sit on a chair. People say that such things are wrong, and in the end, who am I to say they are mistaken? They tell me how to feel, but no threats and no therapy will convince me.

Sometimes I hire models, women who remind me of my sister. Not because they have her exact features or figure. Sometimes it's the way they hold their cup of coffee, other times it might be their chin, their gait. Many refuse—I'm not famous enough to make my offers flattering. After they see the finished painting, they ask, Is this how you see me? Or, Is this how she looked?

•

I remember the afternoon and evening after Rebecca had left town for the second time. Even though I took some tablets, my head wouldn't calm down. I lay on my bed, which still smelled like her, and could feel an army of the tiniest people hack away at my body and brain, cut away pieces, open the insides, and lay them bare. They were in no rush, they were thorough.

It didn't help that I felt like a hostage in my grandfather's house, though the word "hostage" is barely what you would apply to me and my situation. I had agreed to stay, I had seen Maggie and her children and decided not to tell the police. My inaction was monstrous, inexplicable. The right thing was so easy to see, and still, still, how can we testify against those who were always there with us? At eighteen, I should have had a clearer mind, a better grasp of the world. That I didn't is my fault, some sickness within me, some stuntedness that can't be explained. It might be a lack of empathy, it might be just a blind spot, a dead spot, or maybe I'm just using different words for the same symptom—I don't feel enough. It's as simple as that. Or I feel too much, and anything distinct or subtle can't be identified. But that might be flattery. Read novels and you'll find writers with exquisite emotions, a whole doctor's bag of finely crafted instruments. In comparison, my emotions fit into a small child's set of colored building blocks. I'm not subtle, I don't celebrate what I feel.

That night I didn't switch on my lamp, and Opa, when he arrived home, called out only once to me. I kept quiet, I still don't know why he didn't even open the door. Maybe he expected Rebecca to have remained in town. Maybe he wanted to afford the two of us some privacy, though that seems like a strange courtesy from a man keeping his daughter prisoner. He needed me, I'm telling myself. And he needed someone to confide in. He counted on me to be that person. Nobody taught me how to castrate a man.

•

The next morning, I went to school, sat down at my desk, and showed the doctor's note signed by Grandpa. I said hi to Julie, who said hi back, and while we hadn't talked in several weeks and didn't do so that day, it felt like progress. I was a normal kid, I was just a senior in high school. I was good at being normal when I set my mind to it. From now on, I decided, I would need to look completely normal and behave that way. No slip-ups.

At home, I requested to see Maggie. "We need to have a plan," I told Opa. "They should know what's going to happen. We need to prepare them." These things sounded good, but the reality behind those words I couldn't yet imagine. Opa, however, didn't seem to notice my confusion. The words by themselves seemed to make sense to him.

"You're right," he said. "We need a workable solution."

I showered, dressed. He'd promised to wait for me, but by the time I was ready, he was already downstairs. The door to the basement was unlocked. "There he is," Opa said, "and he smells all fresh." He was having dinner with his family. "Come sit."

There was no extra chair, so Greg offered me his, saying he was done anyway. "How was school?" he asked.

"Fine." He'd never set foot in one, knew them only from books. "One day you should come."

He looked surprised, though not in a delighted or joyous way. More as though I had asked him to pee in a cup right there and then. He turned to Opa, who smiled encouragingly at him. "Your cousin's right. Things will change around here."

Maggie kept chewing on a dinner roll. She looked at Opa as if to check if he was drunk. She seemed ready to laugh at any moment, wanted to be in on the joke. She swallowed one last time, said, "Change how?"

Opa's face became very serious before he averted his eyes. "I have cancer," he said. "Leukemia. A slow form of leukemia. I found out a few weeks ago."

There was no audible gasp. Instead, the air was sucked out of the room. There was no sound, just some scraping that seemed to come from inside my ears.

"Cancer?" Greg said at last.

Maggie's eyes melted. Her mouth began to quiver, and wet crumbs of bread fell onto her plate.

Opa played cheerful. "I won't be around forever. I can't keep you safe anymore. You need to learn…that world." His hand flew up in the air, pointing here and there. "Your cousin will be your guide. We'll take it slow—I won't keel over just yet—but we need to get you acquainted with the outside. It'll be a process."

"I want to go." Mayonnaise clung to the corners of Frances' mouth. "When?"

"We'll think about it," Opa said. "We'll think about it." He looked at his family, even glanced at me. "We'll figure it out. I'm very excited. Change will be good for all of us."

I sat among them, looking from one to the other. I was their guide and had already changed the outcome of their lives. Despite all the turmoil, I felt good about the role I had assumed. I would keep the family intact. There was a way out that didn't have to include police and prison. They could count on me.

•

Miles came over half an hour after my call. I met him on the porch to have a few moments alone with him. Neighbors were coming home from work; the day had been warm, and gnats were hovering in cloud columns around the yard. "My cousin's here," I said in low voice I prayed could not be heard from inside the house. "From Minnesota. He's a bit weird. Just to warn you."

Miles emulated my tone, "I think you're actually a bit weird right now. What's the matter?"

"Just don't…don't react if he does something unusual."

"Like what?"

"I don't know. He's goofy. I think he might be a bit slow."

"Special."

"Just don't make him feel awkward."

"Why is he here? School's not out yet."

"Some problems at home," I said. "I think my uncle is getting a divorce."

Greg was waiting for us in the kitchen, an unopened coke in front of him. His shirt showed sweat stains in front, his face was wet. "Hi," Miles said and introduced himself.

Greg nodded. "I'm the cousin from Minnesota. Bobby's son. He's my aunt Carol's brother." His face turned red. I was glad Opa was still at work.

"I thought we could get ice-cream at Fancy's? What do you say?" I jangled my car keys.

"Sure, sounds good," Miles said. "Let's go."

We got as far as the curb. I opened the passenger door to let Miles scamper into the back, and when it was Greg's turn, he wouldn't move. "Not a good idea," he said. "I think I'll stay."

I put a hand on his shoulder. "Come on, it will be fun."

He shrugged off my hand, said loudly, "I don't want to go," then turned and walked back toward the house, his shoulders round, tense. I followed, but he found his way by himself. He steered directly toward the basement door, descended, and disappeared into the apartment as soon as I had unlocked the door. He didn't say another word.

I locked the door once more, waited for my breath to slow. I felt deeply embarrassed, angry at Greg who couldn't even get into a car without panicking. Then suddenly, keys still in my hand, I wondered why I so willingly played guard, why I even kept the door locked. What kind of pervert kept his family imprisoned? Why did I fall into this pattern? What would Miles say if he followed me down the stairs? But no, no. "No," I said aloud, much too forceful. "I'm making sure they are safe."

"What happened?" Miles stood by the car, smoking. "He *was* weird. What's the matter with him?"

I shrugged. "He's afraid of people he doesn't know. I guess his parents wanted him out of the house, but he doesn't feel at home here. Opa is trying his best, but Greg is afraid of everything."

We drove to town, parked next to Ed Glasgow's brown truck. We found him inside, eating a slice of greasy pepperoni pizza. Miles and I bought milkshakes, then sat in my car with the doors open. On his return, Ed put two cases of Labatt's in the bed of his truck. "What are you guys up to? Any hot juicy gossip?" He took a cigarette from a brand-new pack, lit up.

"Opa has cancer," I said, I didn't know why.

"Shit," Ed said. "I'm fucking sorry. He's a good man. What kind?"

I shrugged. "Some kind of leukemia. But he says he'll be around for a while."

Ed snorted. "I still owe him money. Says he doesn't want it. Fixed my arm for free when I broke it some years back. Your grandpa is a saint."

I nodded, then watched him get in his truck and drive off.

"What an asshole," Miles said. "Mom says he raped and killed Linda Brand. Acts like it never even happened."

"Maybe he didn't do it," I said.

"Right. He takes an underage girl to the beach and she disappears, and he has nothing to do with it. How likely is that?"

"They never found her."

"Fuck. You can make a corpse disappear in the woods no problem. Anywhere. Just go down a logging path, dig a little, done. Takes an hour at the most. Nobody will ever find a corpse here. Zero chance. Doesn't mean he didn't do it."

"I guess," I said. But I wasn't thinking about Ed Glasgow anymore. My Opa the nice guy, my Opa the saint. By now he'd be home descending the stairs to visit his family.

•

Greg's meltdown gave Opa a new argument to not rush into things. Even before the aborted trip to Fancy's, I had noticed Greg's vacant stares, panicked glances when the outside world was mentioned. He had never even watched a sitcom before. The world was a basement, and his direct relatives were all the people he could handle. My presence in the basement made him uneasy now, and he'd leave the room every time Opa talked of their upcoming release.

But only a day or two later, Opa brought Frances upstairs sometime after dinner and said, "You want to borrow her for a while?" His tone disgusted me. Frances, though, didn't seem to mind, maybe she was too excited. "You bring her back in one piece."

A minute later I helped her into the car. "Where are you taking me?" she said after we had backed out of the driveway and were headed toward town.

"You didn't look around."

"What?" she asked.

"You didn't want to look around the house," I said.

"Silly!" She turned away from the window to give me an exasperated look. "It's not like he never took us upstairs."

Something about her voice, her easy chiding, made me feel cold all of a sudden, though the heater was working and working well. "You know the kitchen? The bedrooms?"

"Of course. I've even been to your room once, but you had a girl there. She was asleep."

I stepped on the brakes, stopped in the middle of the road. "How often did he take you?"

"Only ever one of us." She didn't mention why and didn't have to. "Mostly me and Mom."

"You know the whole house?"

"Of course I do." She scoffed at my disbelief. "So where are we going?"

"You've been to town?" Fancy's appeared to our left. The store was still open and brightly lit.

"Twice. But only inside Opa's car. He said we couldn't be seen together. He made me scoot down into the footwell."

A car horn behind me made me close my mouth and put the car back in gear. "Where did he take you?" Opa Frank had lied to me. Maggie had almost gotten away, he'd said, the only time he'd allowed her to leave the basement.

"Take me somewhere nice," Frances said.

"But where did he take you?" I asked again.

"Just drive to a place you love."

We left town heading east, toward the shore of Lake Superior. Cars came at us, and I grew aware of her legs rubbing against the black vinyl seat. I offered her a cigarette, and she said the rumble of tires and engine made her body tingle. She gasped.

Had her mom ever mentioned Paul's Grand Prix to her? Was she aware that Maggie had been riding in this car twenty years earlier? Frances' hands stayed on her side, but I couldn't relax. I was too proud, too hurt, too overwhelmed by what I had just learned to enjoy any of this. Still, deep below all the chaos, laughter bubbled up, and I watched Frances turn her head as trees and houses and fields she could not have imagined exploded onto the windscreen. Her lips formed words that I took to mean she was already turning them, us, into a story. I'd been here before, I'd show her. "Is this where you take girls?" she asked.

I thought incongruously of Mom then, not of the woman who was schooling children in Southeast Asia and who might have forgotten that our town, our state, and her own children had ever existed, but the woman in pictures from before Katia and I were born, the woman with sturdy legs sitting atop horses, riding along the shore, long hair adrift. Opa had taken her to a farm on the way to Marquette all through her childhood. She knew her way around horses. Mom had dyed her hair blonde in her unmarried years, and in some of the pictures she wore patterned, sleeveless dresses. In others she didn't even wear shoes while riding in the dunes by the beach. A few photos showed her smoking, and she looked at the photographer as though she expected him to put down the camera at any moment and chase after her. I remembered that girl now. I knew what had happened between taking those pictures in the dunes and the moment after the camera had been returned to the shoulder bag. I knew what had occurred after that and how Mom had betrayed those moments by settling for a life with Dad in our small town. And when I looked over at Frances, I imagined her to be the girl who looked back at the man taking pictures, laughing at him, daring him to follow.

Once we got closer to the shore, I turned onto a rutted path. The car shook and shuddered, and Frances' hands pushed against the dusty dashboard. Her eyes didn't blink. The vents were on high and blasting her with heat. Scraggly gray and black bushes surrounded us after I unlocked her door and pulled it open. Her black, patent-leather shoes—where had they come from?—sank into the dirt. She followed me toward the beach.

The water was a mess of grays and jagged lines. The smell seemed to frighten her. Night clouds had been fitted low across the skies, and there was no moon. No stars were available. The wind whipped Frances' hair and blew sand in my eyes. She laughed, I thought. I bared my teeth and took off my coat. I took off my shirt and gestured toward her. She stood there like a coat rack, stiff and prim. I stepped out of my boots, unbuttoned my pants. Only then did she drop her coat, her skirt, and walked toward the water in pink panties and a white bra. I scooped her up in my arms and walked into the choppy waves. I felt myself laughing now. Ugly sounds gurgled up in her throat. She beat my ears with her fists.

•

I would castrate my grandfather. That would be his punishment. To the boy I was, this seemed like the only logical course of action. I was convinced I should kill the old man myself, but I couldn't face spending the next years or decades in prison. If I castrated him, he would refuse to tell a soul about it, of that I was completely certain. He wouldn't call the cops on me either, because what man would admit to castration? No, above all, he would want to save face. He wouldn't be able to hurt Maggie anymore and in time, his cancer would finish him off. His family could finally live safely above ground.

This seems like a very crooked form of justice when a stop

at the Sheriff's office would have solved the situation once and for all. To me however, it appeared to be the only plausible solution. I wouldn't go to jail, I would punish the old man, and I would make sure that Maggie and her children were taken care of and would not be dragged into court proceedings and in front of TV cameras. It seemed so logical a plan, I set out to make it happen.

I hadn't been inside Opa's shed since the days of making love to Julie. I needed a knife, something sturdy, something sharper than the old Swiss Army knife my dad had given me. I found a rusted scythe, a rusted machete. While going through the contents of the shelves mounted along the unfinished walls, I hit upon an old duffel bag. I took it to the front of the shed to have a look at it, and as soon as I had unhooked the straps, old letters poured forth. They fell to the wet ground, and in my astonishment I didn't move for several long moments. The envelopes had hotel addresses printed on them, some had been made from random sheets of paper, it seemed. All were addressed to Maggie Holmstrom, sent to Opa's address. On the backside, invariably, was only the sender's first name. Paul.

My surprise might only have reflected my naiveté. Yes, I knew that all the stories Opa had told me about Maggie running off and living in California were fabrications, but I had never bothered to investigate what I had been told about Paul, even though I was driving his car. If everything I had learned from my family about Maggie was a lie, how could the story about Paul selling his car to Opa be true?

I stuffed the letters back into the duffel bag. After another half hour of searching the shed, I still hadn't found the right knife. Opa hadn't returned from work yet; my hands smelled sour and burned.

That night, after the old man had finished watching the news, switched off the lights, and walked upstairs to his bedroom, I emptied Paul's bag onto my bed. He had been methodical, had always recorded the date, and even added the name of the city he'd been writing from. After taken them from their envelopes, I ordered all thirty-seven of them chronologically. The biology book on my desk lay opened to the chapter on protein synthesis, but by midnight I still hadn't touched it.

Most letters weren't long. They described the jobs he took, talked about the general changes in his life. Only rarely did he talk about the few months they spent seeing each other in our town. How fresh Maggie's face had looked—polished like an apple, a doll, a rainy windshield—and how raw and wondrous it had felt to be close to her. The letters didn't detail much, but again and again he came back to the day he'd left town without her.

The day of Maggie's graduation, he had waited in his car outside in the parking lot. She had promised she would elope with him that day, but never showed. He'd already accepted a new job near Phoenix, Arizona, as far away from our town as was possible for him—she'd made him promise to leave the Midwest forever—and he waited with his engine running for two more hours after everyone had filed out of the school's auditorium. He never considered driving by her home and confronting her. She'd lost her courage, he believed, chickened out. He was young and angry and left town with squealing tires.

Yet in the following years he regretted his hasty departure and sent letter after letter to her. He never received an answer, and because he was traveling a lot, might not have expected one. For nearly ten years, Paul kept writing. A first marriage ended in Tulsa, a second never really ended; he lost sight of her near New Orleans. He'd written on motel stationary and on pages torn from cheap paperbacks. His handwriting was oddly elegant, barely legible.

I lay on my bed staring. Every month, every day lay open still. The styrofoam tiles on the ceiling, surely intended for better insulation, had been placed haphazardly, ignoring the structure, the obvious connective patterns. The result was disconcerting, mean. I opened my lips and they formed lines from

Paul's letters. "You made my heart blast off like a rocket…your hands were so unconcerned…write me what you're missing! Is it my arms? There are two Pauls, and the one who counts is always with you." Opa Frank had collected the letters. Had he shown them to his daughter? Read them aloud to her? Opa wouldn't have kept the letters from her, his cruelty wouldn't allow that. And what had Maggie made of them? Did she hear my car's engine every morning when I left for school? Had Greg and Frances described the car to her?

Paul's duffel was sitting on my desk chair now, and I couldn't bring myself to inspect its contents until after I had slipped into the kitchen, pulled a bottle of rye from one of the cabinets, and poured myself half a tumbler. I hardly ever drank liquor, I had no taste for it, but my next step required something I couldn't name and that I didn't have. Back in my room, I sat down on the floor, drank half the reddish liquid, then pulled the bag into my lap.

It was made from green canvas, with brown leather patches in the corners. There was one large compartment, and a smaller one in front with an extra zipper. That one held an expired passport and a plastic pouch of photographs, some chewing gum, and some change. The photos were mostly old, some black and white shots of a boy who I took for Paul sitting under a Christmas tree, standing like a tourist next to a Harley Davidson, blowing out candles on a birthday cake. The colors of the other shots had badly faded, turning everything orange. These were of Paul and Maggie. In one of them, they stood in front of Fancy's, large sodas in their hands. One was of them kissing, their heads at a weird angle; maybe Paul had taken it holding the camera himself. There was one picture of Maggie sitting cross-legged on the hood of the Grand Prix. She was lithe, head cocked, self-assured, and regarding the photographer with bemused skepticism.

The large compartment of the duffel bag, where I had found Paul's letters, held mostly clothes. A pair of ratty sneakers was at the bottom, white, made from pleather. Two pairs of jeans, a few t-shirts, two flannels. I held them out in front of me, I sniffed them, but they didn't hold any information, only smelled like bag and dank shed.

I opened the Dopp kit and looked at a cheap razor, some toothpaste, small bottles of shampoo and lotion taken from hotel rooms. The towels too, seemed to come from hotels. A few knick-knacks were wrapped in socks and underwear. A ceramic cat, a glass pipe, a bracelet made from glass beads, a few hair bands. At the bottom of the bag lay a manila folder with magazine clippings. These were glossy photos of women in fashion shoots, and when I laid them out in front of me, they all started to look like the girl in the faded photographs.

I drank the rest of the whiskey. I put all the items back in the bag, zipped it, and stored it under my bed. I didn't have to look through Paul's belongings to know what they meant, but only now, near sunrise, drunk and with a headache forcing my left eye shut, did I allow myself to pull those thoughts I had kept out of sight into my room and in front of me. I switched off the lights, soothing the pain for a moment. Opa would soon come down the stairs and start to make coffee. Down below, Maggie and her kids would sleep for maybe another hour or two. Our time held no sway over them.

Like the faded pictures, I laid out my thoughts carefully. They were simple, and maybe you couldn't even call them thoughts but only responses to what I had discovered and how the duffel bag and its contents fit into what I already knew.

That Christmas after my parents had left town for the first time, Paul had returned to find Maggie. When nobody had opened the door, he went to stay in the Karvonen's motel. How odd that he and the woman he was still in love with had stayed at the same place for a night or two, unaware of each other, separated by only a few walls. They could have met at the breakfast bar or outside in the parking lot. Maggie might have spotted the Grand Prix before Opa returned her to the basement.

At some later point Paul must have talked to Opa and demanded to know where Maggie was. Maybe he'd had an idea about what kind of man Opa Frank was. If so, he should have been more careful. He should not have waited in his motel room for Opa to arrive; he should never have met him alone. Frank Holmstrom had not purchased the Grand Prix, nor had Paul left town on a Greyhound bound for California. Paul was still here. Did Maggie know?

10

There are some strands of our lives that are neat and organized. They won't give you any trouble. Others never quite end. They start and stop, start and stop, they just come back and refuse to be over, even though in the later stages you've given up on them. You lose your belief that they will end the way you dreamt of when they first started. You doubt they'll ever end, because they don't progress. They develop their own dynamic, but no arc emerges, nothing so pretty.

A few days after my trip with Frances to Lake Superior, I stayed after class had let out. I needed to make up for an English test I had missed while Rebecca had been in town. Mrs. Clark had handed it to me that morning and asked me to turn it in by four o'clock. I had an hour, plenty of time. Rainwater running down the windows obliterated the street outside. For a while, I felt soothed by the outsized sounds. I was on a ship out on the lake, the shore out of sight. I had left Opa and Maggie and Frances and was on a journey north, days away from landing in Canada, where no one would be able to locate me. A few minutes before the hour, I left the classroom. The hallways were empty, but near the auditorium I found Julie sitting on a table. Her leather boots were dark at the tips, the shoulders of her coat soaked too. Her hair was made from worms.

"Hey." She waved at me.

"Julie." I held up the sheets of paper as an explanation. She smiled her sweet smile, as though she were embarrassed for the two of us, and then we laughed.

"Is Mark coming to pick you up?" I said.

She nodded and wiped at the water still dripping from her hair.

"I can wait with you." The chair I pulled scratched over the tiled floor. I winced at the sound.

"I don't think that's a good idea," she said. "He'll be here any moment."

"It's okay," I said. "Unless you don't want to. Or is he going to beat me up again?"

She shook her head; I was allowed to stay.

"You're wet. Did you walk here?"

She nodded. "Yes," she said. "That the English test?"

It was my time to nod. I was making a fool of myself and didn't know how to stop. "Why are you meeting him here?" I said.

"I can't go home."

"Oh," I said as though I understood.

We sat in silence for a long time. School wasn't so bad after classes were over and everybody but the cleaning crew had left. The smell of bleach was overpowering. Julie checked her watch, a white digital one, every other minute. Every other minute the hallway where we were sitting turned a bit darker.

"Maybe I should go," I said. "Everything okay?"

Julie looked at her watch again.

"I can drive you home." I pulled the car key from my pocket. "You and Mark okay?"

"Of course we're okay," she said. "Of course we are."

What I did next still surprises me. It wasn't me perhaps, who got out of his chair and took the four or five steps toward Julie. Maybe the ship on board of which I had been crossing Lake Superior had sunk and I was stranded in a strange town and suddenly understood why the girl in front of me hadn't moved in a while or asked me to leave. I sensed that Julie waiting alone in this hallway might create an opening for me. I wasn't me. I can't have been me. The boy who approached Julie had nearly drowned. I stooped and kissed her on the lips. She didn't reciprocate but she didn't budge either. Then I went back to my chair.

"What was that?" she said.

"A kiss," I answered.

Maybe she noticed my presence for the first time that afternoon. She looked at the wet tips of her boots, ran her tongue over her lips, as if I had left a residue. A moment later she got up and her hand reached for mine. We didn't speak on our way to the art room, which everybody knew couldn't be locked. At the back, divided by glass doors, existed a smaller space the art teachers used as a break room. Smoking was allowed. Julie dropped her bag on a wide cabinet holding art prints, then she turned to me, arms at her side, her eyes searching for mine in the half dark. The light was the color of mice. "You want me, don't you?" she said.

Her underwear had a stain, her bra cut into her sides and back. A patch of fine, nearly invisible hair grew on her lower back. Stubble covered her thighs. She'd been wearing a skirt, so she pulled down her woolen pantyhose and crouched over me on the big armchair where Mr. Kauffman sat and smoked and critiqued our drawings.

Julie smelled of Kleenex and rock salt and ice and sleet. Sounds slipped from her lips, and they refused to form my name. I said hers and filled the cold air around us with those letters. It's all I had. What I felt was beyond what I had learned, but her name fit all of it. Only her name could hold what I felt.

"Now you've made a mess." She sat on top of me for another minute or two, then got up to wipe herself.

"Why did you tell him?" I asked. "Why did you tell Mark about us?"

"I didn't."

"He said you told him everything. Before he tried to beat me up."

"He knew everything. What was I supposed to say?"

"How did he know?" I asked.

Julie balled up the napkin and dropped it to the floor. She

shook her head, wet hair covering her eyes. Her legs were trembling. "It's late," she said.

I followed her out of the room wishing I could slow down her steps. If we had opened a window and climbed into the flowerbeds below, we could have reached my car without being seen. Yet I had no words, no offer to make. Moments later, we spotted Mark in the hallway outside the cafeteria.

"Hey," I said.

He nodded. Julie ran toward him and put her face on his neck. Her hands tore at his shirt, his shoulders.

"I'm sorry," he said. "I..." He stopped to look past her at me, eyes squinting.

"Later." I walked past them down the hallway toward the side exit, unlocked the car and felt my breath fill my sides and the cold lick my face. Tell me what you're doing! Is it good? Tell me, who are you thinking of? Is it me? I didn't stop crying until I parked in our driveway.

·

On days I came home from school while Opa was still seeing patients, I walked the grounds right up to the tree line. I looked for loose dirt, a telling bump, while at the same time chiding myself for believing Opa could have left such obvious traces. Paul might lie buried outside of town, along a logging path, as Miles had suggested, or up near the coast. He would never be found if Opa had taken precautions. Still, at the time of Paul's disappearance, it had been the middle of winter, and only the county roads had remained open. Opa had already been stranded once. How far could he have driven, how deep could he have dug to dispose of the body?

At times I knew what I would find eventually; it felt as real as anticipating dinner. Most often, though, I couldn't stand searching for more than ten minutes. It didn't help to look at the house and contemplate how many times I had seen it through our old kitchen window without knowing that my aunt and cousins were hidden away in the basement. Even now, holding the spade in my hand, what I knew to be true seemed impossible. Families were not supposed to be kept prisoners, men like Paul were not supposed to be buried in the backyard. These things must not exist.

Up until then, I had not visited Maggie without Opa Frank being in the house. But one morning in late April, I went into the kitchen while he was having coffee. His white shirt was impeccable, his gold Rolex sliding in and out of his cuff. He looked trustworthy, a man fully in charge of his life, capable of caring for others. Then I noticed that the shirt was askance. The buttons didn't line up correctly with the buttonholes. His fingernails were longer than I had ever seen them.

"Why don't you give me the key today?" I wore sweats and my Miners hoodie, no socks. I could smell my own breath.

"The key?" he said.

"Frances can use some company. Maybe I can start teaching her and Greg the stuff we're learning at school. She might be interested."

"Isn't she a bit young?"

"There's no such thing as too young," I said. "She's smart." If this argument sounded strange, sleazy even, that was fine with me. The more horrible Opa thought I was, the better.

"I might want to wait on that."

"You don't trust me." I pointed at his shirt front. "We need to make progress. This whole situation needs to make progress. It's not right and you know it. If I had wanted to rat you out, I would have done so weeks ago. You need to trust me."

He stood up, looked at his shirt. I thought I saw his cheeks reddening. He unbuttoned the lower half, redid the row without turning away. "I was in a hurry," he said as though to convince himself.

"I want to see Frances. I need to spend some time with her."

"Okay. Okay, we'll try it tomorrow."

"No, we'll try it today. Your fly is open too."

It wasn't, but when he realized I had fooled him, he pulled out the key. "Okay. We'll try it today. We'll try it."

"We're cut from the same cloth." I hoped my face was as inscrutable as his.

"I'll get takeout for dinner," he finally said. "I'll be home at six."

·

I didn't take Paul's duffel bag with me. I pocketed the glass-bead bracelet and the ceramic cat, checked that Opa was indeed gone, and went to the basement. I'd be late for class. The key in my hand had a neat red plastic cover, so you could easily pick it out from the others on the chain.

The overhead light was turned on in the kitchen, and a second lamp near the hot plates had been switched on as well. No matter when you entered the apartment, the lights were always switched on. Frances sat at the table in an oversized Mickey Mouse shirt cut like a wifebeater, so when she got up to greet me, I had to avert my eyes. "Hey you." Her voice was tender. "Don't you have to be in school?"

"Is your mom here?" I was so serious, I didn't realize how stupid my question was until Frances burst out laughing. Maggie appeared in the door a moment later. She seemed surprised, flustered. She turned her back on me, then must have decided that her pajamas would do, and finally faced me again.

"Can I talk to you for a moment?" I asked.

"Sure," she said.

"Frances, can you leave, please?" This wasn't how I had envisioned the moment, but the reality of three people hidden in the basement killed all my plans.

The girl looked crestfallen, suspicious, hurt, all at once, but she left without another word. I felt disgusted with the power I held over this family; I felt excited by it. Nobody had ever listened to me before, not ever.

After we had taken two chairs opposite each other, I pulled out ceramic cat and bracelet and put them in front of Maggie.

It was a gesture gleaned from TV shows and crime novels. I expected my aunt's face to crack, I wanted her to break into tears.

She hardly looked at the objects on the table before gazing up at my face. "Gifts? For me?" she said.

"I found those," I said. "Do you remember them?"

Maggie picked up the bracelet, ran her fingertips over the beads. "I think I might have had one of these before. Where did you get this?"

"And the cat?"

She shrugged her shoulders. "What is this?"

"They belonged to Paul."

"Paul?"

"Paul Deming." I was nearly shouting.

Maggie shrank back. "He gave you these?"

"Did Opa never tell you he came to see you? He was here, looking for you!"

"Why would he do that?"

It was me who cracked. My voice couldn't handle the situation. "He was still in love with you. You wanted to run away with him, and he never got over you. A few years back, he came to look for you. He was still driving his old Pontiac. He kept it because it's the car he drove when you guys met."

She looked stunned. Her chin retreated into her flesh. "That was a horrible car. I hated that car."

"But you wanted to elope."

She picked up the cat. "Maybe I gave this to him? Did he give it to you?"

"You don't remember?"

She shook her head. "That was a long time ago. It looks kind of familiar. Maybe I bought it for him in Marquette?"

"You went to Marquette?"

"A few times. I was a wild one. And Paul was fun. Where is he now?"

I hadn't thought about that question. Or better, I hadn't

anticipated the moment she would ask it. I thought she would beseech me with questions, pull out her hair, plot against the man who had imprisoned her and forced her to have his children. In my mind, I had already told her many times that Paul was dead, murdered by her own father. I had played the scene in my mind time and again—after giving her time to compose herself, I would lay out my plans on how she and Frances and Greg would be set free. We needed to be careful, we needed to make sure Opa couldn't harm them. We needed to be patient, careful, cunning.

I hadn't made plans for the Maggie sitting across from me at the kitchen table in her basement. I didn't know that woman, couldn't imagine her. I became certain, however, that she would report my behavior to Opa. Her allegiance was to him, not me. It was Opa she trusted, Opa she followed. In that moment I grew afraid of her. "Paul left. He thinks you're in California," I lied.

Maggie snorted. "Frank told him I was in California? And he believed that?"

I took cat and bracelet and put them back in my pocket. "Don't tell Opa I showed you."

"What did he look like?"

"Nice. He didn't have much money."

"I told him I wanted to leave town. He wanted to get married in Vegas." She said this not to me, she seemed to be pulling thoughts from her mind like worms from wet soil.

"I wanted to ask if Frances is interested in me teaching her."

"He didn't tell me about that," Maggie said. "He didn't say a word about Paul. He's still jealous." A moment later she called Frances. Her daughter appeared still wearing the oversized Mickey Mouse shirt. "He wants to teach you. What do you say?"

•

At six, Opa came home as promised with takeout from Anthony's. I said I wasn't hungry, so he left a styrofoam container for me, took the red key from the kitchen table, and went downstairs. I waited for an hour in my room, until it was dark and the streetlights illuminated my room. Opa had not yet come back upstairs. Maybe Maggie had kept quiet about the souvenirs I had shown her. Maybe the topic hadn't come up yet. My betrayal hung in the house like the smell of fried food, mixing with whatever Opa had bought at Anthony's.

The air was surprisingly mild, like running into an old girlfriend who doesn't mind giving you a hug. You recognize her smells, you stay a moment longer in her warmth, and still you don't trust her. You're in love again, at least for a short while. My face contorted in sobs, no tears wanted to come.

I drove up and down Grant Street twice before I parked the Grand Prix two blocks away. In our town, everybody had an old muscle car in their garage; nobody would notice the old clunker. It wasn't tricked-out enough, not well-kept enough. It wasn't the one everybody wanted to own. The left side of my jaw was aching from a sinus infection.

I had a view of Rebecca's old window. It was lit—maybe her mother was moving her quilting supplies into her daughter's room, maybe she went through Rebecca's school essays to help her explain what had happened to her daughter. Maybe Mr. Karvonen was lying on Rebecca's bed weeping.

Nobody expected me at home. Opa might not reappear before morning. I was supposed to be silent. I was supposed to protect his little family, protect myself. Paul was decaying somewhere in the back of Opa's house. I would find him, I made that solemn promise. I would lock my bedroom door tonight. I'd be better off that way. For once, my future didn't feel hazy at all. It vanished that night, while the light behind Rebecca's window kept burning.

11

Julie's parents stood on our doorstep the next evening. Her father pushed Opa aside to swing at me and broke three fingers on the door frame. Mrs. Krag cried the whole time. She didn't wear a coat even though the day had turned chilly. Her hair was straight and long, and even back then I knew from the pins and combs that she hadn't been to a hairdresser in a long time. Thin strands of gray curled up on top.

Mr. Krag cursed, swore, crossed himself, swore again. Julie was pregnant, Mark wasn't the father. She swore it wasn't him. He had beaten my name out of her. His knuckles looked terrible. His fingers were delicate, his nails nicely clipped and smooth.

An abortion was out of the question. The Krags were Catholic. They lived in a tract home on Dogwood, in a neighborhood that had once belonged to the mine. Now the trees had matured and hid how shabby the houses were, how thin their walls. Only fresh paint held them together.

Julie was college material, her dad said, shaking his delicate fingers as though he could fix them that way. College material, he said. Julie was smart, funny. She was college material he said over and over again. I couldn't make sense of his face, his tiny nose, his deep-set eyes, a face in which all the bones had disappeared. None of his features had passed on to his daughter. Her mom, however, was a smaller, older version of Julie despite the gray in her hair. She had the same hooded eyes, the same high forehead. Once Opa had asked them in, she sat next to her husband and said, "Terry, Terry," whenever his voice threatened a new outburst.

He never tried to hit me again. I hadn't tried to duck;

punishment, even undeserved punishment, I would have accepted greedily. But why did I readily admit I was the baby's father? Was I so vain that her pregnancy made me proud? I'm asking myself that question again and again, but there's no neurological pathway to the old me. The old me has taken a different road; we haven't caught up in too many years. My memory no longer provides me with all the pertinent details, and the pieces I do remember seem meaningless. They don't offer an explanation that would hold up to the scrutiny of even a distracted listener.

It was true, I longed for Julie, but that feeling had short, stubby legs; more and more often I managed to outpace it. Still, I believe I *was* flattered. In her misery, Julie had named me as the father of her child. This suggested love and small, tender sentiments laced with warmth, something as intimate as a used Kleenex, a smelly sock. Making love to her in the art classroom, I had wondered who else she was seeing; I had not for a second regarded Mark as permanent.

I nodded to whatever Mr. Krag said that evening. I told him I was sorry but that I loved his daughter. I would marry her to save her from shame and gossip. Those words came easily, as though I had memorized them my whole life. They were so ridiculous, they had to be true. I felt satisfied, utterly contented once those words had left my mouth. I sat there with a smile—I was the one Julie had picked. Her child would be my child, no matter who the father might be.

And for the first time in his life, Opa Frank seemed proud of me. After my confession, he offered the Krags whiskey and poured me a glass too. I hadn't had any plans for my life, I was barely going to graduate. Now I'd proven I was a man after all. "Of course they'll get married," he said with grim cheer. He was upset, furious, and yet I had never seen him so excited.

I can't remember what happened later, after the second whiskey. The Krags stayed for another hour or so, haggling with Opa, making plans, setting dates. I don't remember much at all.

I just looked from one to the other, amazed at how easy it had been to finally be recognized. Until now, I hadn't even existed in the Krags' life. They knew my face and nothing else. Should they have seen me getting out of my car on Grant Street the previous night, they wouldn't have greeted me or known my name. But twenty-four hours later, I owned a family. I was part of something bigger. I would get married and raise a child. I wouldn't share Paul Deming's fate after all. The Krags and the upcoming wedding would keep me alive.

•

In school, Julie was the only news. I doubt she had talked to anyone, nor had her parents wanted the pregnancy to become public, yet once I had locked my car in the school lot, the first of many hands that day patted my back. "Nice job, man! This time, Mark will kill you!"

I got high-fived all day. While Julie was a top cheerleader, I was only a second-rate receiver and had done well for myself. I had shown that my dick worked just fine. Opa's approval had felt important, my new importance in the classroom filled me with disgust. For myself, for Julie, for Mark, for our small school in our small town. I couldn't get enough of it. All the strange glances, all the whispers at my back, were so many pastries lined up on a picnic table. How many could I devour before I got sick?

I heard the word from Mark's mouth first. "Slut," he called Julie when I picked her up in the afternoon to drive her home and he was dealing weed to some seniors. She was a possession now, the life in her belly needed protection.

We weren't living together and wouldn't be any time soon, not before the wedding anyway. We didn't even talk to each other much. Not in the car, not during the familial meetings to plan our wedding. That first time I dropped her off in front of the Krags' home, she pushed open the door and said, "I'm never going to fuck you again." I nodded and pulled away from the curb.

Mark didn't kill me, he didn't have to. He was killing Julie instead, and before long the pats on the back stopped and were replaced by hostility. Two weeks after the first visit from the Krags, Julie dropped out of school. Teachers had agreed she could take exams at home and graduate high school despite missing the last few weeks. The word 'slut' had become the only word used to describe her. Repeated again and again, a shower of bullets—after two weeks Julie was a sieve; all her resolve had been drained. She dyed her hair black cherry.

•

After the Krags' visit, Opa took me to the basement and told his family I was getting married. "Soon," he said, "real soon." I watched Frances' reaction, her eyes shutting off, but it was Greg who asked, "Can we go? I can be the cousin from Minnesota again. This time I won't be afraid."

Sometimes, we follow a pattern of thought for so long, we forget that there were other possibilities along the way. We're so in love with our own logic, we commit the stupidest mistakes. Before Dad left he frequently told a joke about a farmer who, because his wife has died and his farm is far away from town, tries to mount his cow. He gets up on a stool behind her but every time he's about to enter her, she takes a step forward, and he has to move the stool and try again.

Suddenly he hears a loud crash, and as it happens, a small plane has crashed not far from his shed. The only survivor is a young, beautiful woman, and after the farmer carries her from the burning wreck to safety, she opens her eyes. "You saved me," she whispers, "I'll do anything you want." And the farmer says, "Please hold my cow."

Greg's question, naïve and asked with little excitement, erased any expression from Opa's face. I sat very upright, as though I needed to bolt, and my face reddened. Opa had raised the specter of a time beyond the basement himself when he had allowed me to join his little family, but what was revealed to us all in that moment, I like to think, is that there never had been any reason to keep the family imprisoned in the first place. By sheer force and routine, Opa had made Maggie and her kids follow his pattern of thought. They'd long ago given up thinking about the outside world. They had just stopped asking about it. Even the occasional escape—driving to the beach at night—wasn't a release, just a break. No witnesses.

"What?" Greg said after a long silence. "Just think about the food."

"Yes," Opa said in a low voice. He was losing his grip on his flock. "Yes, that would be something, wouldn't it?"

•

The Krags insisted that one Sunday after church I take Julie out for lunch. It was their idea of us getting to know each other. "You should learn how to respect each other," her mom told me. "There's not much that can derail our daily lives. That's what I believe. We are made one way, and unless we are removed from our surroundings by force or killed, we absorb the shocks we experience. Even bad marriages," she added. Her husband had given Julie a list of topics she needed to raise with me if we wanted their support.

Julie's belly was round and tight by then, gone was its softness. I bought a six-pack and large orders of chicken wings and fries at Fancy's, and just after leaving town we turned into a logging path off the county road and drove until the trees turned black—we had reached the area of last year's wildfire. There was no one else around. I spread my coat on the blackened ground and we each drank three bottles of Old Milwaukee. Julie only ate one wing but both our fries. She said, "Look, I ruined your life."

I shook my head. "You didn't."

"Yes, I did. And before long you'll notice and start hating me." She paused. "It's not yours, you shit."

"I know," I said. "I can help raise it."

"Fuck off, asshole," she said. "Fuck off."

But we kept sitting on my coat, and the sun behind layers of clouds was warm enough that she took off her jacket and lay down after she was done with fries and beer. She burped and laughed. She let me touch her belly because, "You're paying for it. At least for now. How does that make you feel?"

I didn't answer. I rested my hand on her belly, and it wasn't the same belly anymore. It wasn't Julie anymore, not the Julie I had smoked weed with and who had fucked me on the hood of the Grand Prix. Her skin appeared different. The lines of her face had changed.

"Should we read the list?" I said.

"Sure. What the hell." She pulled the crumpled piece of paper from her skirt. "Here, you read it."

"*What will he do after graduation?*" I stopped. "He? They haven't even written down my name."

"You desecrated me. Do you want them to love you?"

"I'll work. I can find work. I'll pay for our expenses. Maybe Opa will give us some money." This was the first time that I thought about the monetary value of what I knew about him. It was a sudden idea, and I felt ashamed for thinking it. I felt ashamed for not having thought of it before. Quickly I read the next question, "*Where will you live? The apartment above the garage is too small for a family.*"

"I'm not going to live with you," Julie said. "No way."

"Then why am I reading this list?"

"Not my idea."

I stood and lit a cigarette. The wind was warm, and still, it seemed to tug and tear at my skin. I couldn't get comfortable.

She wasn't looking my way, just staring into the sky with empty eyes. "We don't have to raise the kid. Not together anyway. Maybe not at all."

I blew out the smoke and watched her sprawled on the ground, her mouth falling open, something yellow stuck in her front teeth. I thought of Opa taking Maggie to the basement, adding rooms to the small apartment as the years played out. Such enterprise, such cunning. Oma Anna had lived her life unperturbed above.

"Think about it," Julie said. "Some people can't have kids. They'd give anything to raise a healthy boy or girl."

"How do you know it's healthy?" I asked.

"They usually are. Our family has good genes. I mean, we're not that pretty, but everyone lives to their nineties."

"How about Mark's genes?"

"Why do you want to raise a baby? You're fucking eighteen. It's not yours."

"Because it's..." I didn't finish my sentence. I finished the cigarette and walked off down the logging path. Maybe she'd come after me, she might get scared alone by herself.

The ground was still muddy, never mind the warm weather. I slid and slipped along the side of the path, listening to birds and wind that made the charred trees creak, watching ragged and ink-stained clouds hurry after one another. I couldn't quiet my thoughts, I couldn't be still, I couldn't stop walking. I stepped off the path, not caring if I got lost. The fire had eaten bushes and brush, the trees no longer looked like trees. Spidery shadows painted into the sky they were. The ground was still black and brown, and I stared at what lay ahead of me and didn't see the burned-out van until I could touch it. Lying on its roof, the vehicle had caved in front, and the windows had burst. It was a VW camper van, a tourist van. Nobody in our town would have bought such a thing. How old it was, I couldn't say. The paint had disappeared, all the sheet metal looked rusty. I crouched to look inside, crawled closer toward one window opening, only to jump up again and run. I stopped seconds later, because I finally grasped that nobody from inside the van would follow me.

There were two. It might have been a man and a woman, but I couldn't tell from their features. How old they had been or where they had come from, the fire had eaten away.

I imagined the two bodies in the van as a young couple, camping in the forest because they had no money and didn't want anybody to observe them. A camping ground meant lots of families, children crying and screaming. That's not what they had wanted.

A van so far into the logging area was a strange sight, but stranger still was the charred tree that stood a good ten steps away from the overturned vehicle. By some coincidence, only portions of its branches were gone. Some still had leaves on them, though now they no longer looked green. Two folding chairs lay under its branches, the fabric burnt away, the metal skeletons rusty. A metal folding table lay on its side. Leaning against the tree trunk stood a large mirror in a silver metal frame. The glass had cracked but, despite fire and long winter, not fallen away.

What use had the couple had for the mirror? Space in the van had been limited. Had they watched each other eat and drink before it got too dark to even make out each other's silhouettes? I looked at my own cracked image, my burst, reddened face. The sky behind me loomed like a grimy window obscuring the sun. I raised an arm to swipe at it, wipe it clean. I wanted to see the blue beyond, which on clear days seemed so impossibly high and pristine, you could feel that if you just went far enough you could escape the pull of our town and Lake Superior and go somewhere else, where there were no streets like Dogwood and Grant and Mackinac Lane.

•

It took me an hour to find my way back. Julie sat in the car smoking my last cigarette, her bare feet hanging out the window. Her feet still looked the same, they were still pudgy and friendly, while the rest of her was full of soot. Soot nested in her every wrinkle, every small line and wrinkle was dark with it.

"Who wants to buy it?" I asked after I had turned the key and the engine blubbered to life.

"Pete. The owner of the hardware store. I think their baby died. Was stillborn. Died early. Fuck, it's just dead, and he wants another one. He asked Mom."

"He asked to buy our baby?"

One of her pudgy, friendly feet kicked my knee. "It's not yours."

"But you told your parents it was."

"He didn't say 'buy,' but Mom isn't stupid."

"And she's fine with it?"

"Dad can't know."

"How are you going to keep it a secret?"

"I'm not going to stay here. In this town."

I put the car in gear and eased down the rutted path. The light had turned from benign to prickly. I put on my cheap sunglasses and they didn't help one bit. Maggie had said that same thing in this same car some twenty years earlier. Would I be willing to take Julie down to the basement so she wouldn't disappear?

"So you're having the baby elsewhere, your mom is giving it to Pete, and your dad never finds out?"

She didn't answer, she didn't need to. "Where am I in all this?" I asked.

"You're a fucking moron." Julie started to cry. "It would be so much easier if the baby were yours. I'd sell it in a second."

•

I came home and showed Opa the list Mr. Krag had given Julie. He put on his reading glasses, studied it briefly, and said, "Let's sit in the backyard."

The wind had calmed down, the light was falling below the pain threshold. Two peeling Adirondack chairs and a metal folding table was all the yard furniture we had left. Opa opened a new bottle of rye. The air was thick with moisture and moths and crickets.

"Now spring has come and winter's dead. The snow has gone so draw a breath." He paused for effect, or just to watch the lines dissipate. "You need to leave. It'll be better for you." He poured us large glasses of rye and added some ice he'd carried outside in a soup bowl and a shot of Ginger Ale. Then he didn't say anything more for a while. We clinked glasses, and I took a sip, and after the third, my feet seemed to leave the ground, and my head unscrewed from my body and felt a lot lighter too. I laughed, not knowing what could be so funny.

We sat in silence while the air cooled off. The second drink kept me warm.

Opa said, "This town won't forget. You don't want to raise your child here. Let's forget the wedding for now. We'll go to the Justice of the Peace and have the church wedding later."

"Later," I echoed. "Where do I go?"

"I've already called a friend in Saline, down south. You could start working in his body shop."

Maybe my mouth stood open, maybe my expression had turned to what Katia had called 'the potato face.' "I phoned just in case," Opa quickly explained. "I'm mean but not stupid. Decent pay and nobody would know what happened. They'll love you," he added and poured himself another drink. "You're doing the right thing. She's a keeper," he added in a low voice. "Son of a bitch, she really must like you."

"They won't know what happened?" I repeated his words.

"Shotgun wedding, stigma, Mark and his friends, the insults."

I watched the ice disappear in the brown liquid. I'd never burped in front of Opa. "What will happen to Maggie?" I asked.

"What will happen to Maggie," he echoed. "For now, I'm doing okay. When my health deteriorates, I'll let you know. You have your own family now, you need to think of Julie. She can't find out about your aunt."

"No, she can't." And there was the thought again—how much was my silence worth? How much money would he hand me before I went down to Saline? What would keep me from making a call to the sheriff and have him check out Opa's basement?

"Of course I'll help you pay for a decent place." He had read my mind, and I didn't enjoy the feeling of floating in my chair any longer. What would he do to me before I had the chance to leave town? What story would he make up about my disappearance? That I had skirted my responsibility to Julie? I had gotten cold feet and abandoned my child?

"What about Paul?" My voice didn't sound drunk, I thought.

"What about him?"

I tried not to look at the shed, the weedy grass covering the backyard. "He came to look for Maggie and you lied to him."

"Yes," Opa said. "What else could I have done? Once we've committed a sin, it makes our decisions for us."

"You could have confessed. You still could. You could go to the cops. Everything would be over."

"Are we talking cops again? We've agreed on a year to set things right. You have my word. You'll be busy raising your son, but I will make things right."

"A son?"

"The way she looks. I've seen many pregnant women." He noticed his misstep right away, I'm certain. His statement included his own daughter. We fell quiet together, then remembered our glasses full of rye. By now it was too cold in the yard without wearing a jacket. Opa only wore a flannel, and I the Miners hoodie. But there was something else I had to ask. It was an all-important question. I didn't need the answer, but I needed to know how Opa would answer it. "And Paul is out there looking for her in California?"

"Yes," Opa said after a second.

I nodded. I had missed the moment when things had shifted. Or maybe they hadn't shifted at all. I had been stupid to ever trust Opa. I understood why Julie's baby made him so happy and why he was now suggesting I leave town. Maybe he had been scared enough after the run-in with Mark to share his secret with me, or maybe he had hoped I would not be appalled by his crime and help him care for Maggie, Frances, and Greg. But ever since taking me to the basement he must have regretted that decision. He couldn't wait to get rid of me.

"Okay," I said. "Okay, I'll leave."

12

After I told Julie about the job down south, she nodded. Her face didn't betray any emotion. "The sooner the better," she said. We sat in the small living room in her parents' house, on a blue sofa covered in dog hair. The TV set was an old black-and-white one, the kind I remembered from my childhood. Rabbit ears sat on top, right next to a small china figurine of Jesus in gold-embroidered white robes.

"Opa will help us pay for an apartment," I said.

"Great."

"We'll do the real wedding later."

She didn't give a sign she'd even heard me. She still wore pajamas in the late afternoon, baggy things that didn't betray her shape, and bright-red winter socks with small bells on them. The afternoon light was leaving the windows, filling the room with shadows.

"We'll just take some clothes and a few small things. We can buy everything we need in Saline."

She lowered her torso onto her knees, pulled off her jingling socks, and stared at her toes. The paint was chipped, her nails jagged. "I won't stay with you for long. I'm going to leave you as soon as this one pops out."

"You said you wanted to leave town."

"I didn't say you were my first choice."

"Then why…?"

"Because Mark's parents have plans for their son, and those plans don't involve girls with babies. Girls from families like mine, babies that pop out before marriage. If I told them it's his, they'd disown him."

"He's a dealer."

"A businessman. His parents own half of Grant Street."

"And you're okay with him abandoning you?"

"He didn't abandon me."

"He really believes…"

"I did cheat on him. I'm so fucking stupid. But I'm not stupid enough to live happily ever after in some fleabag. If I get into your car, it's not because I want to start a family with you."

"You wanted to get out."

She didn't answer for a while. Instead, she stared some more at her feet, then at the darkness rushing toward us.

"I need to get out. Just don't count on me to stay."

"You've made a deal, then," I said. "You're going to sell it."

She got up, stood very straight in the small living room with its low ceiling, then walked toward the back of the house without a word.

•

I locked my room at night; Opa Frank must have noticed. I still went to school in the morning, kept to myself during lunch break, endured break-ins into my locker, put baby shoes and used diapers in the trashbin. In the evening, I prepared my own food. Once I was gone, what would keep me from making a call from a phone booth near Interstate 94? Yes, Julie had given Opa a way to get rid of me, but my absence would also complicate his situation. I would no longer be under his influence.

Before leaving town, I needed to make sure Opa could never again attack Maggie or Franny. The task frightened me, but it had to be done. I saw no other way—and maybe the method I chose appealed to me in its depravity. It appealed to my sense of guilt over not going to the police. If I couldn't do the right thing, at least I could do the drastic one. It fulfilled a sense of vanity, self-importance, and justice. Not the police would be in charge of Opa's fate. His grandson would be prosecutor and judge. Afterwards I'd be free to raise or sell a kid, live with a woman who hated me, leave for New York and marry my sister. None of this can be measured in logic.

When I try to remember the young man I was, I endow him with abilities to reason he didn't possess. Reasoning is still not what gets me from one day into the next, and how much worse that boy fared, for he was a boy, when making plans all these years ago. I watch him every now and then from a great distance. His naivete and cruelty horrify me; something that I admire has since disappeared. This older self has not been able to hold on to the sense of urgency and necessity, this older self is no longer so narrowly focused that anything appears possible.

Dogs had always roamed our dirt roads. You only needed to walk a mile or two and eventually you'd run into a pack of them, half-wild, always interested in picking a fight. Past Ed Glasgow's house on Mackinac Lane a young bloodhound came bounding toward me and, a moment later, put his paws on my shoulders sniffing my face. He was too big, I told myself. But I was determined and after his curiosity had been sated and he'd gotten back on four legs, I crouched down.

I swear there was no one else on that dirt road. The house the bloodhound called home stood a quarter mile away, surrounded by mature trees. Old trucks and cars stood to the left and right of the driveway, some bulwark against intruders. I heard no engines, no tires coming in my direction. The dog seemed bewildered by my sniffing sounds, intrigued by my nose in its fur, or maybe stiff with indignation. How would I hold his head down? How would I get close enough without being shredded by paws and teeth.

I watched him trot off, shaking.

•

Thursday after school, a set of empty moving boxes stood on the porch. It was a warm day, maybe the hottest of the year so far. My shirt was damp from driving a car without AC and protested noisily when I tore it off the vinyl. Opa sat at the kitchen table in shirtsleeves drinking a beer. "I thought it might make things easier," he said.

"I'm not taking anything."

"You might rethink that. And in any case, we can store your stuff in the attic. Franny can have the room once she…well, you know. She won't want your things, I'm sure."

"Why don't we bring all of them up here tonight?" I shouldn't have asked, I shouldn't have pushed him now that I had decided his fate. Still, the sight of the boxes made me hate him, made me hate leaving the town with Julie and a kid that wasn't mine. Or was it? What if Julie's story was true, after all? We'd had sex all winter, and how was a woman to know who the father was? I heard stories of women 'knowing' but I doubted Julie could tell. What if the kid was really mine and Julie gave it away to be raised by strangers? I'd been chewing on that for the past few days, and my anger bubbled up now. "Why don't we make dinner and have everyone up here?"

"That wouldn't work."

"Because someone might come? Someone might recognize Maggie and ask where she's been all these years?

"They don't know this world."

"You brought her up here yourself. Franny, she told me."

"A mistake."

"How did she get away?"

"Franny? She never…"

"Maggie. That winter. You had received a letter from Paul, hadn't you?" I was spilling what had given me power. I was too angry to be afraid, too angry to let my face betray that I had slipped up.

The benign resignation on Opa's face tightened into something impenetrable. "What letter?"

I recovered quickly. "He said he had called many times, but that you hadn't answered. He must have written. Or he must have written Maggie that he would come and see her."

I could see that my effort wasn't convincing Opa. He got up, not looking my way. "I'm not bringing them up here. They are not show ponies. They are not your play things. I have sinned greatly, but I have also treated them as human beings. That's hard to understand, especially for someone so…"

"Below your expectations?"

"Your words."

"Did Mom know Maggie was down there? Is that why she left?"

Opa stopped on his way toward the hallway. "I expected too much of you. For that I am sorry. Of course I should have known it would upset you. Repulse you. I will take care of this. Before I die, I will take care of my family."

"Take care of them. Make things right. Why don't you just open the door and say, 'Here you go. You're free. Here's money, you can keep the house. I'm going to Mexico so the police won't jail me."

He'd been staring at the ground in front of him, as though listening patiently to a baby scream or a dog bark. Now he said, "Because I love them. Because I can't give them up. It would kill me."

I avoided him for the next two days. When I heard his steps or smelled coffee, I ran from the house or barricaded myself in my room. I grew fearful. I wouldn't eat at the house anymore. Whenever I closed my eyes, I saw Opa walking toward the shed out back. Yes, the letters were gone. Paul's letters were gone. I saw him turn toward the house, his mind working visibly behind his eyes. I could see the subtle shifts as he planned his next move.

•

I found him sprawled in front of my door, one morning when I was already late for class. He was lying on his stomach, face bent awkwardly to the side. I couldn't believe my luck—Opa was dead. He was dead and I hadn't even touched him. The cancer had worked faster than even he had anticipated. In a minute, I would release Maggie from her prison, I would sell this house, leave Julie, and move to New York in search for Katia. My hometown was losing its grip on me. I could smell Katia in the brief moment before I heard him breathe. It was a rasp, something that spoke of pain and confusion. I got down on my knees beside him. Sirens were coming our way, and only then did I grasp that he'd had the time to call an ambulance.

I rode in back with Opa, an EMT hooking him up, making sure he didn't die on the way to the hospital. Opa looked green; I'd never seen that pallor on a human face. Gone were the sharp edges of his face. The strong jaw appeared slack, the skin thick and loose. I pitied him and refused to touch him for fear of ending up the same. I wanted him dead, I feared he wouldn't make it and leave me to sort out his mess.

Our hospital was a one-story building at the edge of town. Critical cases were flown by helicopter to Marquette. Opa had often joked that if you had a serious illness, you wouldn't leave the hospital alive. Scissors had been left inside patients' stomachs, two doctors had resigned after being accused of malpractice. Procedures had been performed on the wrong patients. Babies and mothers had been mismatched.

How difficult would it be to loosen a cord? To remove a breathing tube? To press a pillow onto Opa's face? My hands were sweaty, I hadn't taken the time to put on socks and was still wearing my pajama pants; I plotted against him. I was shaking at the thought he might die.

•

By noon, he had been wheeled into a private room. The doctor, a short woman with a Spanish accent, told me he would recover quickly and, in all likelihood, fully. A mild stroke had felled him. She asked me about stress, workload, eating habits, and I answered as though Opa had led a particularly boring version of our town's life. I had no explanation for what had happened. She nodded at my answers and revealed that Opa suffered from hypertension. Had he ever taken any medication against it?

I shrugged my shoulders. She nodded some more and

smiled vaguely. "Doctors," she simply said. "To carry the torch, you don't have to be enlightened."

I couldn't make sense of her words. "He's got cancer," I said.

Her brows met. "What kind?"

"Some kind of leukemia," I said.

"Chronic lymphocytic leukemia? Your grandfather has reached the age where this is a possibility. We'll have a look. Once he's awake, he and I will talk. Don't expect too much of him too soon."

After she'd left, the only sound was the ticking of a wall clock, light slanting into the room without brightening it. The body on the bed didn't feel alive, no smell or heat emanated from it. I grew restless, I hadn't even brought a book. I hadn't eaten yet. How long would I wait for Opa to wake up? All my observations and questions turned selfish, petty. Why couldn't I muster more generous thoughts?

A nurse entered carrying Opa's belongings. She deposited pants and shirt into the closet and put a plastic bag with loose items in a drawer. As soon as she had left, I went through that bag and retrieved Opa's keychain.

He opened his eyes hours later while I was fingering the tubes that led to two plastic bags, liquid dripping into Opa body. I hugged him immediately, not caring whether I smothered him. My face was wet when at last he could hold open his eyelids. "Where are we?" It took me and him several tries, then I understood the slurred words. "The hospital," I said.

"You're here." He sounded astonished.

"I have to leave soon." Not for a second had I thought about Maggie, who still didn't know her father had suffered a stroke.

"They're out of salt," he murmured.

•

I retrieved a shovel from Opa's shed. Where would I have hidden a corpse? It had been winter, the ground frozen. I walked into Siberia, let myself get lost for an hour, contemplating the possibilities. I searched the ground for strange signs without hope of ever finding them and slowly made it to the railroad tracks. Someone had camped there, built a fire. The ground was still burnt, a few pieces of clothing lay discarded. A hoodie, two pairs of jeans, a single black sneaker. Empty tins of tuna and beans had been picked over by birds.

On my return, I rounded the house. Opa would not have dared digging on the side adjacent to Mom and Dad's old house, but the neighbor to his left had grown tall hedges. In any case, a man digging a grave in the winter didn't look so different from someone shoveling snow. The closer to the house he buried the corpse, the less suspicious it seemed.

I walked the length of the house, spotting the shaft that provided what little light Maggie's apartment received. I was growing excited in the most quiet way. I had dropped a pebble into a well and was listening for the sound of it hitting the water. I walked up and down, listened and listened. Long after sundown I began to dig.

.

I didn't visit the basement after I awoke in the same clothes I'd worn the previous day. I showered, I took my time. I fired off insults, I cheered myself on. Whenever I fell silent, my arms and legs started to shake, so I kept raising my voice. I had no script, no clear goal, no means to protect Maggie after her release. And whenever I thought of flinging open the basement door and saying, "Run," to the three prisoners, the next image in my head turned out to be Opa wearing a green jumpsuit in jail.

If I gave Maggie my car, would she leave town? Did she remember how to drive? Had she ever learned? Putting them on a bus wouldn't be enough; Maggie had unlearned the world, and her children had never entered it in the first place. I would have to leave with them and abandon Julie. I would have to leave without any of the people in our town ever finding out what Opa had done. Would he follow us? Would he attempt to reel us back in? How would I keep Maggie safe? How would I feed a family? I followed that same train of thought all morning. I tried to find new turns, new paths, new reasons, but however hard I tried, I ended up in the same place. I didn't go to school, instead sat on a kitchen chair listening to the noises inside Opa's house. None came from the basement.

The man I am now of course sees possibilities. There were ways and means available to even an eighteen-year-old. After all, wasn't it better for Maggie to be free and broke than to be clothed and fed in a basement? And my face still turns red every time I let myself sink into my memories and wonder why the former me was so afraid of being questioned by the sheriff and going to prison. I was to blame for my inaction, still am to blame. I failed Maggie every day I stayed in Opa's house.

Around noon, I did go downstairs, having filled two plastic bags with groceries from the pantry and refrigerator. I unlocked the door, set down the bags just inside the kitchen, and locked the door behind me again. Nobody had heard or seen me. It had been so easy. I would attend afternoon classes. I changed my clothes a second time that day.

In the early evening I received a call from the doctor. Opa's health had declined. They weren't sure what was happening. The doctor's voice sounded worried, she said they would be running tests.

"Is he going to die?" I prayed I didn't sound hopeful.

"We're going to run some tests," she repeated. "If his situation worsens, you'll hear from me or my colleagues."

•

I hadn't expected Julie to call. She said we needed to talk, said her father wanted to talk to me as well. I drove out to their house on a Wednesday, and Mr. Krag came to the door and invited me in, told me to have a seat on the blue overstuffed sofa. This time, the dog hair had been removed.

He poured me a cognac, sat it down on a coaster in front of me. The coffee-table looked shiny, immaculate. "We might be old-fashioned." Mr. Krag took a seat in a matching overstuffed armchair. His hair was thin and freshly combed, as shiny as the table. I was waiting for the second part of that sentence, yet it never came. He lifted his glass, waited until I had lifted mine, then said cheers and fell silent again.

A minute later Julie appeared in a sleeveless patterned dress, teal and red, her eyes red and puffy. She sat down cross-legged on the other armchair and looked at neither of us.

"Julie told me you found work with the trolls. That's good."

"It's a good opportunity."

"We won't let her go without a wedding." He smiled as though to apologize, but his eyes weren't in it.

"Opa thinks we should just go to a justice of the peace now and have a church wedding later."

Mr. Krag looked at his cognac for a long time, seemed to derive a silly pleasure from watching the liquid swirl in his glass. "That's not how the Krags do things," he said.

"Opa says they won't forgive us. He says we'll never fit in."

"He should be talking to me. It's my girl's wedding. We're giving her away."

"Dad," Julie said. "You're not giving me to anyone, and I'm not some cut of meat."

"This is not what Mom and I wanted your life to be."

"Well, I screwed that up, and now we have to come up with another plan."

Mr. Krag's face turned purple and under his thin hair his scalp turned a bright pink. I thought he might hit Julie, he might hit me, but he never stopped swirling his cognac. "We'll have a real wedding," he said very softly. My arms broke out in goosebumps.

"When?" I asked. "I'll have to leave right after school ends."

"We'll make it work," he said. "We'll let you and your grandfather know. The kid cannot be born without the blessing of the church." He sighed heavily afterwards. His naked feet stuck in cheap pleather slippers.

Julie walked me to my car. "I thought about things," she said.

"Oh?" I had no idea what she meant.

"I'll come with you. I'll live with you."

"Okay." It seemed too easy. I had returned to the Krag's house without hope, meaning to cross one thing off my to-do list before leaving town. "Has the deal fallen through? Does Pete Saeger no longer need a baby?"

"Don't be an ass. I've changed my mind. I want to do what's right."

"But there won't be a wedding. I have to leave soon." Then I told her she needed to be ready and that we might only have a few days left, maybe a week, maybe less. I would call ahead, come to her house, rev the car, and she needed to get in. By morning, we'd be near our new home.

"You're such an idiot," she said. "Rev the car? You can just show at my door."

"I'll honk. Just be ready. We'll need to leave."

"You're a drama queen." Then she stepped forward, grabbed my face and kissed me. She stuck her tongue all the way down, as though she were going to suffocate me. She wiped my mouth afterward. "Just get me out of here."

·

It was Frances who dropped the bar of chocolate she'd grabbed from the grocery bag, sank to the ground like a second-rate actress and whimpered, wiping nose and face with her burgundy sleeve. Maggie stayed calm at the news of Opa's stroke, asked the questions. Greg kept walking through the apartment, from one end to the other. He'd never crossed a lawn, had never seen a football field; Opa Frank wasn't interested in boys.

"I should be there for him," Maggie said. "I should go and visit him." She was sitting on a kitchen chair, feet firmly planted as though she might storm out of the basement.

"It would upset him." I had locked the door behind me, though in that moment I couldn't have said why. "It's too risky."

"Who would recognize me?" she said. "We can go together.

You have the key now." Beyond her head, beyond the wall behind her head, I had filled in Paul's grave.

"You won't be down here much longer at all."

Greg stopped in front of me, his bulk too close to my chair, his head hung, his neck a broken branch. "What do you mean we won't be down here much longer?"

"You'll be free very soon."

"Very soon?" Maggie said. "Why not now?"

"Opa is in the hospital but he'll be back in a few days."

"Why not now?" Maggie asked again.

"Why not now?" Greg echoed. "You took Franny on a drive."

"What are you getting out of this? Is it Franny you're after?" Maggie's voice wasn't combative, her face still open. She meant every word of that question.

I had the keys. I had no argument. It was hard to focus on what I had intended. "He'll go to jail if anyone sees you. Do you want him to be in jail?"

Frances interrupted her crying, shook her head. Maggie didn't react at all. Maybe she was thinking about the options, maybe she thought about kitchen knives, my soft belly.

"You won't be down here another year. He won't be able to harm you anymore. Just don't tell anyone."

"Who would we tell?" Frances said.

My skin was burning. I closed my eyes not to be looked at anymore.

Frances insisted. "I'd like to visit Dad. Nobody knows me. You can take *me* to the hospital."

"You look like Katia."

"I'm not Katia. And Friday is my birthday. We can't celebrate without him."

That last bit stunned me. I don't think I'd ever considered that someone locked up in a basement could have a birthday party.

Maggie didn't pay her daughter any mind. "Does Frank know what you're saying?" she asked. "What exactly are you saying?"

"Never mind," I said. "Just be ready. You won't be holed up here forever, I swear." I got up, bumped into Greg, who yelped and retreated. Nobody came after me. I unlocked the door, passed through. I locked the door.

●

I found a small blue leather suitcase in his closet, filled it with socks, underwear, pants, a shirt. I packed his toiletries, which, for a doctor, appeared neglected and poor. I told myself I was in charge.

On the drive to the hospital, I kept the windows down, the air a drunk lover, all mouth and hot hands. New York was a day away. There, I would locate Katia, and her face would fall silent, her arms would squeeze these past months out of me, and with a large gasp I would come back to life.

A different doctor answered my questions this time. He was taller than me, with a plump face and cheeks full of stubble. He chewed on his fingers and leafed through Opa's chart. "We were worried he'd had a second stroke, but we found nothing. Dr. Garcia told me you said your grandfather had cancer. Did he tell you that? Did he diagnose himself?"

I nodded.

"Did he tell you what kind?"

"Leukemia. The old people kind."

"We were looking for a connection, took blood tests, did a CT scan. We didn't find any cancerous cells. In about two days, I think you can take your grandfather home. He won't be able to work for a while. Who will be looking after him?"

"I will look after him," I said. "No cancer?"

He shook his head. "You in school?" He looked at his bitten cuticles, noticed me watching him. "You have any other relatives?"

"They've all left town."

He adjusted his horn-rimmed glasses, glanced one more time at the damage he'd done to his cuticles, then jammed the hand into his coat pocket. "We'll give you instructions. He needs to take his medication, take it easy."

"Two days?"

"Maybe three. Dr. Garcia will discharge him when she thinks it's safe."

Someone had opened the curtains, and bright beige light took up all the space in Opa's room. No flowers stood on the nightstand; I hadn't brought him a single thing until today. His hair was oily, the hospital gown exposed his slack neck. I held up the suitcase for him to see, then slid it into the closet next to the sink. "You'll be out in two days," I said. "Just in time for Frances' birthday. You didn't have another stroke."

"How are they?" His voice was faint but clear.

"They're asking about you," I lied. "They're worried."

"Nonsense," he said. "I'll be fine." He tried to sit up but couldn't.

"Maggie and Frances want to see you. Should I bring them?"

His mouth opened. I waited until it had closed again without making a sound. "You don't have cancer." I had to force out these words, because what they meant was already slipping from my mind. Just being in Opa's presence was enough to alter everything I knew, adjust it in so many ways. "You lied to me. The whole time. You lied." I wanted an answer, I wanted him to tell me more lies. I wanted him to say how much he loved me, how much he cared about me, how important I was. I needed someone to say those words, anyone. But he and I, we were past that. No, we'd never even been there, had never stopped at that place. He wasn't into boys.

I took his left hand and placed the watch on the rubber strap inside. Opa glanced at it quickly, before averting his eyes. He didn't drop the watch, he didn't hide it under the covers. He didn't fling it at me.

"I cleaned it," I said. "It's still working."

Opa's head sank back onto the pillow. He stared toward the ceiling.

"They call it a Pepsi bezel. The colors have faded, though."

"What do you want?" he whispered.

"It's an automatic. 150 meters water-resistant. Paul was still wearing it. You didn't buy the Grand Prix from him."

He closed his eyes. He knew what I'd done and how I had recovered the watch. I said, "You had no intention of giving up your family, you just wanted me gone." After that, there was nothing left to explain.

I spent some of the money from his wallet on groceries, pocketed the rest. It was only a matter of days before I would have to leave town. Once Opa would be back at the house, everything was in place. My grandfather was a sick man, he wouldn't be steady on his feet.

13

I went to school, endured the strange looks and laughter. I had to remind myself they were meant for the boy who was going to get married and raise a child. The teachers didn't call on me, and I had little idea what the equations and diagrams they scratched onto the blackboard were saying. It was the first time I felt something like peace. I still knew the rules here, and most students followed them. In a few short weeks they'd be donning gowns, and their parents would shower them with love, cars, and money. They'd go to Anthony's or have barbecues in the backyard. Boys would lose their virginity and leave for college in the fall.

Miles barely noticed me. During lunch, I saw him with Heidi Bergman who lived across the street from the Krags. Later, in chemistry class, he bragged about how mature she was. She knew how to do it. Wearing a denim jacket and black suede shoes, he said he was growing out his hair and ready to head off to Detroit and start a new band, and I thought, he's ahead of me now, he's leaving me behind. I'll never catch up.

I stopped at the supermarket and bought a cake. I bought bags of candy. I bought silly hairpins and socks. I bought a potted flower and a stuffed bear. Frances' birthday; Opa would be back and we would have a party.

I bought a bunch of tulips and drove over to Dogwood. Julie had cut her hair once again. The dark cherry was gone. Instead, she'd bleached her hair white, then drawn leopard's fur into it in black. Her belly stuck out under the tight dress she was wearing.

I gave her the flowers. She sniffed them, tore off one head and stuck it into her mouth. "I'll name her Tulip." Her bare arms were round and heavy. She hadn't shaved her armpits.

"What if it's a boy?" I said.

"It was a joke."

I looked at her, trying to read her face like a public notice. "Saturday evening. We'll leave Saturday evening."

"I'm sorry for everything." The tulips dropped from her hand, and before I could pick them up, she was stomping on them with her bare feet. "I'm sorry for those too. I'll be ready. Pick me up Saturday night. I'll keep it together, at least until we get there."

"Okay," I said.

"I'll need some new clothes. I'll be bigger than a house."

"I'll buy you clothes."

"That was a joke too."

I stared at her face until she stuck out her tongue and laughed. I turned, walked back to the car. She waved at me with the ravaged flowers in her hand.

•

Ed Glasgow's truck stood in front of Fancy's, so I slowed and parked across the street. Inside the store, he was talking to Marv, the night cashier, who was maybe thirty with bad skin and thick glasses and slick black hair in a pompadour.

"Hey Shithead," Ed greeted me. "Want a beer?" A case of Old Milwaukee sat between him and Marv.

I nodded.

"Do it in your car, for Chrissake," Marv said.

Ed laughed, took the case and told me to follow him. He walked around his truck, lowered the tailgate, and cracked open two beers. No matter how dirty his flannels were, he wore them as though they had grown on his skin, as though they needed to be as dirty as they were. "Heard you knocked up Mark's girl."

I sat down next to him, feeling oddly proud and stupid at the same time. "What would you do?" I asked.

"Me? Shit." He looked at the can in his hand, then drank it in one go, crushing the can in his hand afterwards. "I'd deny it. How do you know it's yours?"

"I slept with her."

"So did he, and probably a whole lot more often than you."

That made sense, but that wasn't what I had wanted to talk about. I drank my beer, accepted a new one. "If you found out that somebody in your family had committed a crime, what would you do?"

"Is it a danger to you?"

I thought about that. "I'm not sure."

"You don't rat out family unless they come after you."

"Why not? If they're criminals."

"It's family. The government isn't going to help you when times turn shitty. It's your family that's helping you out. Who's committing a crime? You don't have anyone left. Where's your sister, Shithead? Haven't seen her since she broke up with Scott."

"New York."

"Huh. So I was right about her, then? When are you going to make your exit?"

I was quiet, kept quiet even after he nudged me for an answer. Finally he said, "You always had your eyes on her."

I shook my head furiously. "No way." Then, "What if someone has done something really ugly?"

"You take care of it. But you don't get anyone else involved."

"Take care of it? Like, punish them?"

Ed gave me a look as though I were particularly slow to comprehend.

"What if I can't do that?"

"Then you stay the hell out of their business. Shithead, what could your grandpa possibly have done? He's a good man. One of the best."

"Never mind," I said.

We drank more beers, until he had to piss and walked around Fancy's toward the dumpster. I was slow to get back into the Grand Prix, had little desire to go anywhere, arrive anywhere. I heard Ed's steps on the concrete, he was humming some tune or other. And when I looked up, someone else, someone I didn't yet recognize, someone I hadn't seen approach, stood by the old truck's tailgate. She was holding a shotgun and before Ed had even noticed her, she fired.

•

Karen Brand, Linda's mother, was taken away by Sheriff Gautier. He didn't handcuff her; there was no need. She'd been waiting for him sitting on Ed's tailgate, drinking beers from the case the dead man had bought, one after the other, while people started to gather around her. No one touched Ed, who was missing half his face. No one stepped too close to the shooter, because her rifle still lay across her lap. The Sheriff arrived fifteen minutes later, after Karen had started offering beers to whoever wanted. Only one or two brave souls accepted. She was smoking by then, slumped happily in Ed's old truck.

I waited and watched. I waited until after the Sheriff had left, until after Mike Kalas, who'd owned Fancy's for the past thirty years, had asked the paramedics who carried Ed's corpse away to hand him the dead man's keys and parked the brown truck with the hand-painted flames in the back of the store, near the dumpster where Ed had taken his last piss. I waited, and no one talked to me. Mike didn't shoo me off. Marv didn't come to shout at me. I waited, and only hours later did I start the car, my hand unable to stop from shaking and find the right gear. I was shocked by what I had seen, but that was only part of the uproar I felt. I was scared I wouldn't have the courage Karen had shown, I knew I wouldn't. I was scared because killing Ed had been so easy.

•

I'm afraid of the person I was then; he seems to have been cruelly underdeveloped. I can only guess at what the boy was lacking—he felt so little, he had no experience with the feelings and emotions other people cited and sang about and dwelled on. He knew the words, but the words that had been chosen and used and re-used by generations—he could not fit what he felt into that set of words provided to him. He shouldn't have loved his sister.

I should have reported Opa on the first day he led me into the basement.

I should not have driven out to the hospital to take him back home once Dr. Garcia deemed it safe.

From the outside, we must have appeared like a happy family. I helped Opa into a wheelchair and rolled him into the elevator, out of the elevator and through the sliding glass doors into the parking lot. I helped him into the car and returned the wheelchair to the lobby. The receptionist wished us a great weekend. It was Friday afternoon. The sun was out streaking across the sky, and people were dropping their coats. Colors appeared on their pale bodies. Men already wore shorts again.

I had helped him pack his bag and made sure the dive watch was among the items that left his hospital room. We hadn't talked then, and we weren't talking inside the car. He must have been relieved that it wasn't the Sheriff who came to get him, but he couldn't trust me anymore. He needed to get rid of me, or he might end his life in prison.

"I need to see them," he declared once I helped him up the porch steps.

"We're having a party," I said. "It's Frances' birthday."

"A party," he repeated.

"I bought some things." I'd wrapped the presents and stacked them near the basement door. "I'll be leaving town in a few weeks, and your health is deteriorating. We need to accelerate our plan."

"Our plan."

"We'll have to release them sooner than anticipated. Maggie, your daughter, has returned home from California with her two kids. That'll be our story. They won't tell, people won't pry. The three of them will take care of you."

"Let me rest for a minute. I need to sit down." He walked

gingerly into the kitchen, sank onto a chair. "Please get me a new shirt and a tie. If we're having a party."

I picked a blue shirt and a striped tie. The stairs would tire him out, but I wouldn't let him sleep on the sofa in the living room, nor would I give up my own room. Julie would be waiting for me tomorrow. Everybody needed to be in the spot I had assigned them

By the time I returned to the kitchen, he stood at the sink swallowing something from his open medicine cabinet and washing it down with a glass of water.

His torso, when he changed his shirt, looked very small, boyish even, if not for the wrinkles, the loose chest. The tie he adjusted with trained ease, then let me help him down the basement stairs. His steps were slow and deliberate, his shirt was already wet, but we made it without incident. I unlocked the door and listened to Frances' excited shrieks as I went back to get her gifts.

I cut the cake, I watched the girl unpack the presents and observed her expressions. She wasn't pleased with the socks and hardly looked at the stuffed bear. She did like the cake, though. It was cloyingly sweet, it made my teeth gasp.

After half an hour, Opa leaned close and whispered, "Give us some time." I couldn't imagine what he wanted to say that I wasn't allowed to hear, and I couldn't imagine what harm it could do. I agreed to pick him up in an hour. I even gave him the key, just in case.

I spent that time preparing for what had to follow. I deposited my bag in the trunk of the car, careful not to pack anything that reminded me of Opa, Mark, of Mom and Dad. The things I chose I had bought myself, except for the toy car Katia had given me for Christmas. I opened the Pontiac's hood and checked the fluids. I checked the tire pressure.

By the time I reentered the house, Opa was already back in the kitchen. The key rested on the counter. "Thank you," he said. "She enjoyed the party. It was a good thing you did."

The clock behind him read six-thirty. "It's time for me to go to bed."

"Karen Brand killed Ed Glasgow," I said.

"So I heard."

"I was there. She took revenge on him. He killed her daughter."

"It was never proven."

"She believed it. And she finally killed him. It took guts. She wouldn't let him get away with taking her daughter, killing her. She just went up to him and shot him. People say she won't go to prison, that she was right to do it."

I helped him up the stairs. It took several stops, several intervals of long breaths, but he never asked me to sleep in the living-room or his old office. He asked me for a second glass of water, and I poured him one in the bathroom sink. Afterwards I sat in the living room until the last light had been extinguished in the sky and the streetlights announced themselves in pale orange, turning the world black and gray. Everything happened the way it had to for me to walk back up the stairs near midnight and place the precision steel balls on the top two stairs. I wanted him to fall, I didn't want to be the one who pushed him. I was no Karen Brand. A push wouldn't give him a chance, but the steel balls would. I would be able, so I thought, to manage my guilt.

·

I awoke not from loud thumps and clatter, I had overslept. It was past nine, my stomach rumbling, reminding me of the cake I'd eaten the afternoon before. Frosting still glued my throat shut. I spent the next hour in the kitchen, making sure to be making noise. Opa would rise, walk toward the stairs and take a first step down. The landing was dark, he couldn't see what I had prepared for him. He'd be helpless. And if he survived the fall, I'd be standing at the bottom, knife in hand. My palms were slick with sweat.

At eleven, I finally made my way up. I carefully avoided the trap I had set and then stood in front of the closed door, my heartbeat irregular and noisy.

Opa was still in bed. I could feel the emptiness in the room long before I could see his open eyes, the open mouth. The water glass on his nightstand was empty, as were the three unmarked pill bottles. The room stank.

I stood in front of the bed, too stiff and panicked to touch him. I grabbed the knife, unfolded the blade, yet I never pulled back the comforter, did not pull down his pajama bottoms. What a child I had been for even thinking I could do such a thing. My face grew hot with shame.

I searched for something to feel beside that shame. Fear maybe, or satisfaction. Nothing but bubbles came up from my stomach, which cramped and tied itself into knots. I stood at the foot of the bed for minutes before realizing what the smell was. Then I inched away, closing the door behind me just in case.

I crouched and picked up the steel balls, stuffed them down my pant pockets. I hunted the last ones down the stairs, the ones that jumped from my shaking fingers. At the bottom of the stairwell, I slumped down, sweaty, breathing hard. A deep feeling of joy melted muscles and bones until I couldn't feel my body any longer. Opa had killed himself. Steel balls and knife could be packed away and stored in a shed. I hadn't done anything wrong. It took long minutes for me to comprehend that he had done all the work for me. I was no murderer, I hadn't mutilated my own grandfather.

I called the hospital. The EMTs arrived ten minutes later, without siren or blinking lights. The two men walked up the stairs and confirmed what I had known and carried Opa out on a stretcher. They said they were sorry. The Sheriff's office might give me a call, they said. One of them put a hand on my shoulder, squeezed it. "Tough shit," he said. "You're the guy whose parents are on one of the dark continents, right?" He gave me a form to sign. His colleague stood by the ambulance smoking.

It was two o'clock when the house fell quiet again. This would be the last time I'd go down to the basement and unlock the secret door. Half a year ago I hadn't even known it existed. So little time, I thought.

Usually, we think what is done is done. You can't change the past. It's an illusion we like to honor to the point of absurdity. The last six months had refurbished my past, remodeled it, torn down parts. But most importantly it had robbed me of what I had thought of as my past. There was none left I wanted to remember. Opa's crimes, his wife's acquiescence—how could I ever think of them as Opa and Oma again? My mother had known about Maggie, I was certain now. I'm still certain of it, after many, many years. She might not have been able to articulate it, but she *knew*. Dad must have known as well and left first. Mom left, Katia left, and they will carry with them the proximity to something they refuse to name. Its presence is always there, won't lift even in lighter moments, when the sun is sinking below the horizon and friends are preparing dinner and refilling your glass.

No one was in the basement kitchen. The remains of the party had been left on the table, and the frosting of the leftover cake was runny and yellowed, the air stuffy. I called their names, all their names. I called them twice. I cleared the table while sickness took hold of my stomach. I hadn't eaten yet, the coffee I'd drunk turned my responses into acid. I threw paper plates and forks and knives into the garbage can, a stainless-steel model with foot pedal, solidly made, something Maggie must have appreciated. This was her home. I listened for the tiny noises, the telling signs we often hear beyond what our ears are telling us. I made enough noise for four in the kitchen, I put on fresh coffee. This I still can't explain.

They were resting on Maggie's bed, where Opa must have delivered his children himself. I imagine him to have been res-olute and tender, overjoyed once again by the miracle of birth, holding his offspring in his bloodied hands, proud as only a father can be. The person he loved most had given him two children. The apartment was becoming too small, and he would expand it in the coming years.

This time, Opa had given them death, just as tenderly, resolutely. The brown bottles were empty, and there was no sign of struggle. He hadn't conned them, hadn't forced them. He'd convinced them there was no better way. The shame—they didn't want to be someone else's freak show. Here, down in this basement apartment Opa had built himself, here they were loved. His love for them would never end.

I locked the basement door. I'd call from down south. I'd call in a few days, once I was out of reach. I needed to leave before Sheriff Gautier could pay me a visit, but I would call once I had reached New York and found Katia.

Why had Opa spared me? Did he not consider me family? Did he not care that I was left alive?

•

In brief moments I forget who I am and what I am capable of. Sometimes I string together enough moments to make them appear like a chain, an uninterrupted sequence, something as steady as the humming in a sleeper car heading out towards California.

Of the many rooms in my mind, I use only a few. Restricting myself has simplified my day-to-day life. The rooms don't have a great view or lots of light, but they allow me not to get lost and mourn what could have been, who I might have been. Someone nobler, someone more decisive, someone better. I'm not better, though I have done little to evoke scorn since I left the small town. What I feel is in my pictures, coded in colors and postures, in half-open eyes and spread fingers. It's coded beyond what the average collector spends on looking at their acquisition. People believe my paintings to be flat and that their range is limited. They don't look hard enough. Just follow the strokes like you follow the lines of a prayer and you'll be overcome. You'll be drawn into a maze that is as complex as anything you're able to grasp. This is what I'm telling myself. This is what I have to tell myself to continue my work.

•

At five o'clock I stopped in front of the small house on Dogwood, revved the engine and honked. After ten minutes, Mr. Krag opened the door and yelled something I couldn't hear over the din. I revved the engine louder and louder but wouldn't get out of the car. Mr. Krag's mouth opened and closed, opened and closed, his face red and contorted. Before he reached the car and his hand could grab the passenger door handle, I gunned the engine and drove off. I haven't been back since.

I think I saw Julie at the Atlanta airport some fifteen years later. I'm certain it was her, with a new husband and a teenage daughter. My heart and my stomach believed it was her. Both failed me, and I lowered my head and put my hands over my face—like a kid who believes he'll turn invisible—until I was certain she had passed without noticing me. I continued in the opposite direction.

I still don't understand why she said I was the father of her child. We had a bond, I told myself. We had a bond, and even though it wasn't love on her part, it was better than nothing. It was the one way in which I mattered to her—I was a small stone in her shoe, snow on her windshield. And then I was gone. She wasn't the most important woman in my life, I can admit that. But to think that I wasn't even anything she wanted to remember still sends heat to my face and makes me close my eyes.

I haven't found Katia. The internet allows me to check up on Mark and informs me about Karen Brand's release from prison, but it is no help finding people who have changed their names, by marriage or other legal means. On opening nights, I still scan the small crowds for Katia's face. I still wait for her hand to come to rest on my arm before the last visitor has left, and her fingers to close around mine. I have searched; she hasn't. Maybe her love for me wasn't as outsized as I wanted it to be. Maybe that love was only mine, reflected but not reciprocated. I daydream of finding her but at night, Katia won't appear for me.

In my dreams, the doorbell of my apartment rings. I open, and it is Frances who rushes toward me, embraces me, pulls my hair. I'm on fire, and there's nothing left to take off, but it doesn't smell like summer so what is it, this new season? I'll show Frances this new season. I'll be here. I'll be right here when she gets back. I think I'll show it to her. Everything. She'll be so tired. When I look this way for long, I think she's behind me, she's had plenty of time to sneak up. I can't miss her. I can't lose track of where I've looked or for how long. I can't get lost, too. Only one of us can get lost. What are you waiting for? It was always you it was always you it was always you. I'll sing it to her when she gets back. What are you waiting for? It was always you it was always you it was always you. That's why I take good care of myself, watch out where I'm going and fear that any drop of rain might kill me.

When I wake up, the sensation is still so strong that I rub my head in pain and wonder. Sounds gurgle up her throat each time I see her, and she beats my ears with her fists.

•

I never sold Opa's house. I pay someone to keep the grounds tidy.

ABOUT THE AUTHOR

Born on the Baltic coast, Stefan Kiesbye moved to Berlin in the 1980s. He studied drama and worked in radio before starting a degree in American studies and receiving a scholarship that brought him to Buffalo, New York. His stories, essays, and reviews have appeared in the *Wall Street Journal*, *Publishers Weekly*, and the *Los Angeles Times*, among others. He is the author of seven novels, including *Next Door Lived a Girl*; *Your House Is on Fire, Your Children All Gone*; and *But I Don't Know You*. *Die Welt* has called Kiesbye "the inventor of the modern German Gothic novel." He teaches creative writing at Sonoma State University in the North Bay Area.